Wolf
Note

First Books Series

Libby Jacobs, *Wolf Notes*
Christopher David White, *Ego Scriptures*
Michelle Moore, *Deepest Blue*

Wolf Note

Libby Jacobs

Rager Media
Akron, Ohio

All inquiries and permission requests should be addressed to the Publisher,
Rager Media, 1016 West Abbey, Medina, Ohio 44265.
First edition 2006
10 09 08 07 06 5 4 3 2 1

ISBN 1-59975-337-5
ISBN-13 978-1-59975-337-9

Manufactured in the United States of America.
The paper used in this publication meets the minimum requirements of American National Standard for Information Sciences—Permanence of Paper for Printed Library Materials, ANSI Z39.48—1984. ∞

Cover image: "Untitled" by Libby Jacobs.
Design by Amy Freels

Contents

For Jack, Shellie, and John

Wolf Note

Sometimes I leave my uncle's house and just drive, letting the clean fingers of the wind tangle my hair, drowning out his choking silence with the purr of the engine. The old Jaguar belonged to my uncle and talks to me with his deep bourbon rumble, the voice he lost with the stroke. He taught me to drive it when I was fifteen and came to live with him after Mother died, was stroked to death. The black leather of the seats still smells like his pipe tobacco, like the smoke from his pipe and the fire in the stone fireplace in his study where I sat each night on the ottoman in front of his leather chair. Every night he brushed my hair and said how different it was from my mother's hair, his sister's hair. Mine he called "chestnut," heavy and straight to my waist. Hers, he said, was finer, naturally curly, strawberry blond. Until he was sent away to school, my uncle had touched her hair, brushed it every night with the same wooden brush he used on mine.

As he brushed my hair, the antique mirror on the wall of the study reflected our faces masked in the shifting light of the fire, his face above and behind mine. His hair and beard were the same chestnut as my hair, but flecked with silver. Uncle's eyes never looked at me directly in the light of day, but were bound to my gaze each night in the haze of silvered glass, as dark and dappled as a guilty conscience, and I wondered if our images left stains on the mirror.

He would brush from the crown of my head to the ends at my waist, one hundred strokes or one thousand. I lost count each night, hypnotized by the rhythm of the strokes. Sparks spit from the burning wood, sparks jumped from my hair that flew up like a wild and frantic thing around my head, sparks like fireflies outside an arched bedroom window. I could hear his breathing and feel my heart and smell the sweet cloying scent of his brandy sheeted on the crystal snifter. He would wet his palms with his tongue and tame the crazy animal that my hair had become and say, "That is enough."

Each night I stood and heard the creak of the leather of his chair as he stood behind me. He would pat my butt with the flat wooden side of the brush, never hard enough to hurt. Never hard enough. He said, "Goodnight, Alicia. Sweet dreams." I walked out of the room knowing that Uncle watched my sparking chestnut hair, my legs, my ass. I wondered how many jagged shards would explode from the mirror if I smashed it with my fists. Each night I closed the heavy oak door and listened for a while to the desperate and lonely sounds he made after I had left his room.

Sometimes I would take a book from his study as I left, prolonging the leaving, wanting him to focus on my arms reaching up, my breasts moving slightly, my hands that he wanted on him clutching a dusty, dry leather-bound volume of history or poetry.

I had never been to school. Mother had insisted that Luis and I study at home. Each one of our handsome and virile young tutors seemed to have two areas of expertise and interest: the subject he taught us, and Mother.

In San Francisco, when it rained, the maid would close the louvered shutters of the sun porch and we would chant our lessons to the sound of water beating chasing splashing in the gutters. My little desk sat beside Luis's bigger desk. I watched him, copied him, loved him.

When I was eleven and Luis fourteen, Mr. Antonelli came to teach us. He took over the tutor's room in the attic and soon the whole house smelled of his thin cigars and coffee and chocolates. Even Mother began embroidering seed pearls of Italian words and phrases into her conversations. He had entered our lives with a battered leather suitcase, a small wooden paint box and two violins. A silver cross dangled on a delicate chain around his neck, hiding in the dark curls hiding in the snowy undershirt hiding in the white linen shirt, Luis and I hiding under the covers. My brother smooth-chested, a path of down on his belly snaking into his pants.

Mr. Antonelli taught us music and art. We were years ahead of other children in mathematics and English. The teacher before him had drilled us endlessly, challenging us to learn more and more, faster and faster, school a game that the three of us loved to play together on the sun porch. He had filled the porch with textbooks, chalk, and pens we dipped reverently into squat bottles of blue ink. But Mother tired of him, I think, or was jealous of the learning and laughter on the porch. One morning Luis and I ran to the room and found some of the books gone. Mother came in wrapped in her dressing gown of Japanese silk, twisted her strawberry hair into a knot at the back of her head, and announced that until we had another tutor, Luis would teach me. Teach me on the porch in the rain and in the sun, reading all the books in the library, she said, except the ones on the very top shelf. But we knew not to touch those. I wondered as she turned away if the butterflies embroidered on the silk might not slip from the smoky fabric into the still air of the porch, but they didn't.

For a month Luis and I studied alone. We read *Moby Dick* and *Jane Eyre* and *The Turn of the Screw*. Luis taught me algebra and we laughed as we unscrambled puzzles to solve for X. Sometimes we wondered at the puzzle of our own lives. X was our father and we could find no formula to help us assign proper value to him.

The week before Mr. Antonelli arrived, Luis turned fourteen. He and Mother and I sat at the long linen-covered table in the formal dining room. We had finished our dinner of steak and "smashed potatoes" (Luis's request) and the maid had cleared away the dishes. It was the first time Luis was served wine with dinner, and his half-full glass of burgundy—and Mother's refilled one—cast stained glass shadows on the white table cloth. Mother excused herself, reappearing in a minute with a glowing birthday cake. Fifteen candles—one to grow on.

She set it on the table in front of Luis, turned his head to kiss him, blushed his lips with the color from her mouth, and told him to make his birthday wish. She sat down again and took a sip of the blood red wine. Luis didn't wait for us to sing to him, just blew out the candles with one breath and sat still with a tight-fisted hand on either side of the cake. "Aren't you going to ask me what I wished for?"

"It won't come true if you tell," I whispered to him. Surely Luis knew that.

"This wish won't come true if I don't tell Mother." I didn't know what the rules were in a case like that.

Mother's hand tightened on the stem of the goblet. "All right, Luis. What did you wish for?"

"I wished to know about our father."

Mother slammed the crystal down on the table. Wine splashed and the stain spread like crimson fingers pointing toward Luis and me. "You both had different fathers. I never married either one of them. Luis was born at home. You, Alicia, were born in the city in a hospital, ripped untimely from my womb. I'm sure Luis can explain that to you later. Your fathers didn't stay around because I didn't want them to stay. I have no idea where either of them is so you can't get in touch with them. My parents died together in a train accident when I was fifteen and left me this house and enough money to take care of us for a long time. Uncle David is your only living relative and you know that he travels in Europe for most of the year. I haven't seen him since before Luis was born. You are both bright and beautiful children and I love you very much." She took a long drink of the wine, draining the glass and reaching for the decanter to pour more. Her tongue peeked catlike out of the corner of her mouth and caught a drop of the wine. "Please cut the cake."

It had all come out in a rush like something dammed up for a million years, like a frenzied genie escaped from a magic lamp. Everything that we had whispered about and speculated about and dreamed about had been thrown on the birthday table as though it were one of my assignments, a bare bones plot summary with none of the poetry, the lyricism, the romance of the novel. Luis pulled the candles out, sucked the frosting off the ends, and cut a piece of cake for each of us. He gave me the piece with the biggest frosting rose. I don't remember what he got for his birthday that year.

A week later Luis and I sat together at his desk, our heads close, hair entangled, pouring over a copy of Shakespeare's *Macbeth*, and I knew that I was responsible for the scar that spread like a crooked grin across my mother's belly. I had seen it once when she called me to bring a dressing gown to her bathroom while she lay in the footed tub, and I had wondered but was afraid to ask what had caused her such harm.

Mother walked into the sun porch with a man in a white suit. He was olive-skinned and almost too handsome. His eyes were dark and heavy-lidded, a neat mustache accented his full lips, the shadow of a beard outlined his jaw. He was not much taller than Mother, but entered the room with the presence of some disturbing, brutal force. I saw the muscles in Luis's neck tighten and he covered my hand on the desk with his hand.

"This is Mr. Antonelli, your new tutor. He's going to teach you Italian and music and painting along with your other subjects." Mother's voice was breathy, as though she had been chased around the house. Her eyes, her cheeks, her strawberry hair glowed brighter than the light playing in the trees outside. "And he has promised to paint a portrait of me—if I can sit still long enough to model for him."

"Your mother is a beautiful woman." His voice was musical with its gentle accent.

We knew that she was beautiful and didn't know what to say.

Mother almost danced to us at the desk. "Classes are dismissed until tomorrow." She closed the volume of Shakespeare. "Come help Mr. Antonelli with his things. Robert went into town to pick up the groceries."

Luis gave my hand a squeeze and released it. "I'm really not feeling well. I might vomit at any minute." He put his hand over his mouth and made a gagging sound. "I'll be in my room." Luis left without looking at any of us.

"I'll help," I said, standing up from the desk, feeling a bit disloyal to Luis. I wanted to see what this man had brought into our lives. I followed him, intoxicated like a winged thing by the rich spice of his cologne.

Mother waited at the base of the stairs while I led Mr. Antonelli to his third-floor room. I knew she would check her hair, her perfect arched eyebrows, her mouth, in the mirror. I carried the violin case and paint box he had handed me. He followed so close I could almost feel the movement of air behind me disturbed by his body.

"Why do you have two violins?" I asked.

"One for my students to play and one for me."

"Could you teach me to play the cello?"

"Why the cello?"

"Because I've always wanted to play the cello." It was a lie. I hadn't really thought about any particular instrument although I had always loved music, but at this moment it seemed like some absolute truth I had just been told.

We had reached the attic and I opened the door to his room. "Do you have a cello?" he asked as he looked around the small room with its dormer windows and single bed.

"No," I admitted. "But I'll ask for one for Christmas."

"Then I'll teach you to play the cello." He laid the worn leather suitcase on the bed, opened it, and began to unpack neatly folded shirts and place them in the dresser.

"Thank you."

"*Grazie* in Italian."

"*Grazie,*" I echoed. "Dinner is at six o'clock. Cook doesn't like us to be late."

I placed the violin and paint box on the small square table in the corner of the room. I almost danced to the door as Mother had done and went back downstairs.

That evening at dinner Luis stayed in his room and Mother had a tray sent to him with a note saying that if he didn't feel better in the morning, she would see that he took a big dose of castor oil. Entranced with the Italian tutor, Mother and

I sat at the table asking him to repeat words over and over, in love with his accent, trying to be the first to pick up the exotic words he taught us. The three of us laughed until Cook stuck her head in from the kitchen to see if something was wrong with dinner.

"May I write to Uncle David and ask for a cello for Christmas?" I asked Mother, when we had settled ourselves and were enjoying poached pears for dessert.

"That's a very big gift."

"I'll write him a *grazie* note," and the laughter began again.

"You may write and mention it," Mother said, wiping tears of laughter from her eyes. The adults stopped laughing and I knew that his leg was against hers under the pristine tablecloth, under the carved oak table. "When do you want to start my portrait?" Mother concentrated on a piece of pear in her silver spoon, bringing it slowly to her mouth, opening her lips and slipping the pear between her teeth, not looking at Mr. Antonelli. Did she know that he was looking at her, her mouth, her teeth?

"We could start tonight. Of course, the light is not good enough for painting, but I would begin with pencil sketches."

"Of course. I would like that."

I excused myself from the table. *Perdono.* I went to my room to write to my uncle.

September 20, 1936

Dear Uncle David,

How are you? I hope you are well. We are all fine.
Mother says that you ask each year what we would like for Christmas. This year I would like to mention something that I have been thinking about for a long time. I would love to have a cello. Our new tutor is a violinist and can teach me to play the cello.
I know this would be a very big gift and I would not expect to receive any other presents for several years. If this is an unreasonable request, please ignore it and choose something for me, as the gifts you send are always very lovely and most appreciated.
Mother says that you may be visiting the States soon and I hope you will be able to visit us.

Addio!
Your loving niece,
Alicia

P.S. Our new tutor is also teaching us Italian and art.

P.P.S. I am enclosing a picture of me that Luis took in the garden last month since Mother says she has not sent pictures of us for a long time.

When I had finished the letter I put on my nightgown, turned out the light and crawled into bed. In a few minutes, the door between our rooms opened, a thin strip of light Luis's calling card, and he came into my room as he had so many nights since our childhood. I raised my covers like the flap of a tent for him, but he sat on the floor beside my bed. I reached out and put my hand on his shoulder. Luis was shaking, I thought with cold, but in the moonlight through the curtains I saw the silver tracks of tears on his face. "We're too old for this," he said, his voice husky from crying.

We heard heavy steps in the attic, from the tutor's room overhead, then lighter steps, dancing. "He is going to begin sketching Mother," I whispered. Luis crawled into my bed.

I lay on my side and he curved his body close to mine, pressing against my back. But this night he whispered no stories to lull me to sleep. His tears dried on our skin as he caressed my hip, moved against me slowly, then faster until he gripped my arms with fingers that didn't mean to hurt and grazed my shoulder with his teeth, and was still. I turned to him and held him until he fell asleep because we had only each other. In the morning he was gone from my bed. I slipped out of my nightgown and ran my fingers and tongue over the spot on the cloth where he had pressed wetly against me.

The next morning on the sun porch Luis and I were given sketchbooks and fat charcoal pencils. Mr. Antonelli piled apples and pears and a lemon beside an old cracked teacup on my desk and we began our drawing lessons, Luis and I, shoulders touching, sitting together at his desk.

Around ten Mother danced in. She usually slept until noon, and rarely came to see us during "classes." She wore white slacks and a black silk short-sleeved blouse and I thought that she and Mr. Antonelli looked somehow like a harlequin couple as he moved toward her in his white shirt and black slacks. Her strawberry curls were caught at the nape of her neck in a red silk scarf. The tutor smiled, nodded, and took the oval tray from her, touching her hand, leaving a smudge of charcoal like an old bruise on her knuckles.

"*Grazie,*" he said, glancing at the cookies and tea with honey that she had brought. Four china cups and saucers clearly suggested that Mother would stay for tea. "The flower brings honey to the bee. Bee, *pecchia*." The last was directed to Luis and me, but the tutor's voice dripped like the sticky gold of wildflower honey on my mother.

I ate my cookie and half of Luis's because he refused the treat even though the cookies were chocolate chip, his favorite, and still warm from the oven. Mother and Mr. Antonelli stood by the window holding their cups of tea and drinking in each other. Luis began drawing again, pregnant pears and swollen apples with nipples like breasts that he smeared with streaks of brown from the melted chocolate of the cookie remains sitting lonely on the plate.

After Mother left, Mr. Antonelli announced that we would draw until lunch. Tomorrow (*domani*) we would begin music. The tutor stood by the door that my mother had passed through as though absorbing remnants of her from the air, then moved to my side to help me round and shade the fruit I had drawn. He leaned over my shoulder, his arm bending around mine, the charcoal pencil in his hand caressing the pear into three dimensions, highlighting and molding it into a ripe and bursting fleshy thing. I could smell the pear, and the chocolate caught on his mustache, and the sun and breeze and starch trapped in the linen of his shirt.

Luis jumped up from the desk, his chair crashing to the floor. He tore his drawing in little pieces and dumped the pieces into his still full teacup. He picked up a regular pencil and ruler from his desk and moved with his sketchbook to the window. He sat on the floor, gazing out at the garden, then began to draw hard and angular designs which looked like plans for a building with hundreds of locked doors and barred windows, architecture for a nightmare. He never again drew the still life arrangements or sad stuffed birds that the art teacher assigned to us. And Mr. Antonelli seemed to know better than to push Luis about the assignments. Luis drew thousands of plans for his castle/prisons in such intricate and impassioned detail that I knew he must have visited there, maybe lived there now in his mind, maybe didn't want to leave.

At lunch Mother called the tutor "Dante" over curried chicken salad and tiny green grapes from the arbor in the back yard, making his name sound like a hungry wicked promise.

After we had eaten, Luis and I went back to the sunroom. From the window we could see Mother and Mr. Antonelli walking through the garden, laughing, laughing together. Luis slammed the shutters closed and suddenly the room was a foreign and mysterious place. "It's time to read a book," he said.

In the stripes of light that whispered through the louvers, I moved like a sleepwalker in a dream that has not yet turned rotten toward my desk to find the copy of *Macbeth*. Over the pear, tiny fruit flies twirled, hovered and twirled, specks of dirt with evil intentions. Luis was by my side. A bee lighted on a pear, nibbled a bit, then sat on the desk, wings whirring. Luis, moving like a shadow, as he had moved into my room the night before, eased the book from my desk and dropped it on the bee.

"*Pecchia*." His voice was a blurred whisper, whirring like the wings. "We're reading a different story today." He turned the book over to look at the smashed bee and laid the slim leather volume beside the fruit. Luis left the room. The legs of the bee still moved, as if it were dreaming of swimming through honey as thick as the air on the sun porch.

I wandered to the window and squinted through the wooden slats. Mother and Mr. Antonelli had disappeared from the garden. More bees sucked nectar from the hollyhocks. They plummeted to the open blossoms, then rose in intoxicated spirals. Luis came back into the sun porch, now stripped of sun. A small book poked out from his jacket pocket. "It's from the top shelf." He cleared the charcoal and my sketchbook from his desk and pulled out a chair for me. The bee's legs had stopped moving. One wing had dropped on the dimpled curve of the lemon and glistened rainbow colors in the too early dusk. The bee's head was an ebony smear on the leather. Luis and I sat together again at his desk and he opened the *Kama Sutra*.

The next morning on the sun porch we had sheets of lined staff paper on our desks instead of the sketchbooks. The cracked teacup and the fruit were gone but I thought I could still smell their heavy fermenting ghost-scent. We learned the notes of the scale, wrote them down, sang them with hesitant, embarrassed voices. Mr. Antonelli taught us musical terms in English and Italian. *Forte,* loudly. *Staccato,* detached. *Decrescendo,* growing quieter. *Fine,* the end. Finally Mr. Antonelli played his violin for us. Dark eyes closed, morning-smooth chin reflected as a shadow on the polished wood, he tuned and played his violin for us and I knew why Mother loved him, or at least I thought that with him there was more reason than with the others.

When he had wiped the rosin from his violin and bow with a scrap of soft velvet of midnight blue, he laid it in its case and tuned the second violin. He held it out to us and I thought Luis might take it and smash it against the desk as he had the book on the bee. Would the strings quiver for a moment as the bee's legs had after death? But Luis took the violin and placed it under his chin, looking at the music teacher with hatred and hunger in his eyes, as if he were starved for this knowledge, as if he might win back Mother's love if he, too, could make the violin sing.

For the next few weeks we filled our sketchbooks—mine with whatever Mr. Antonelli assigned, Luis's with layers and layers of tortured structures—and practiced the violin. I would dutifully play from four to five o'clock before getting ready for dinner. Luis would practice for hours, late at night in the parlor. While the moon traced its curved path beyond the arched window in my bedroom and firefly sparks burned pinprick holes in the fabric of the night sky, I lay in bed and listened to the dance creakings in the attic where Dante Antonelli sketched Mother. From below me came the counterpoint of Luis's violin as he practiced scales and arpeggios and etudes, trying frantically to drown out the other music in the house.

The first week of November a huge wooden crate arrived. Cook's husband, Robert, pried open the thin, splintery lathes and uncovered the cello. A note on monogrammed stationery was woven between the strings. It was addressed to me but I read it out loud to Mother and Luis, Mr. Antonelli and Robert and Cook, who had deserted the salmon mousse and dill mayonnaise in the kitchen to see what had been delivered.

> November 30, 1936
>
> Dearest Alicia,
>
> Here is your early Christmas present. I hope it is satisfactory. If all goes according to plan, I may be returning to San Francisco within the year. (Here Mother lit another thin cigarette and began to braid her wild hair into a thick strawberry plait that hung over her shoulder like a python she was trying to domesticate.) I am growing tired of Europe and this life of constant travel.
> Best wishes for the holidays and the New Year.
>
> Sincerely,
> Uncle David
>
> P.S. I am particularly fond of Vivaldi, although I realize that it will take time and practice before you reach that level of proficiency!
>
> P.P.S. Thank you for the picture. You are your mother.

Mother gave no sign that she had even heard the part about my picture.

Immediately after lunch, I took my first cello lesson. I sat on a straight-backed chair in the parlor, my feet planted on the floor, and spread my knees to accommodate the curved body of the cello. As I pulled the horsehair across the strings, I felt as much as heard the sound, shaking and uneven, but already rich in the promise of music, vibrating and resonating through my legs, up from the bottom of my belly.

I sat there, the shadow of me and the cello shifting with the movement of sunlight on the oriental carpet, until Mr. Antonelli came back into the parlor. My feet were numb, my knees shaking from the unaccustomed effort of holding the cello. He lifted my left hand from the strings. "You must put it away for now. You have played more than enough."

"*Basta*. Enough," I said without thinking about it, surprised to hear that I still had another voice besides the stringed one.

"*Si,*" he said, examining the ends of my fingers and shaking his head. My fingertips were blackened from pressing against the fingerboard, grooved from the strings. "Your hands are still small and the skin just toughened a little from the violin. If you continue to play, you will develop a hardness, *callosita,* to protect you from the strings. But that takes time. You must have patience." He pulled a square of white cotton from his pocket. "From an old undershirt. You need something soft and clean to wipe away the rosin." The cloth smelled of wind and sun from drying outside; under the scent of outdoors hid the faintest spice of his Bay Rum.

"*Grazie.*" I cleaned the glowing body of the cello, wiped the strings and the wood of the bow, and loosened the hairs as Mr. Antonelli had shown us with the violin. I wanted to take the scrap of cloth to bed with me but was afraid that Luis might find it.

It was about this time that I asked Mother how her portrait was progressing. She tilted her head like a curious cat, as though I might somehow know more than she did about it. "Dante says he is pleased but he won't let me see it until it's finished. It seems to be taking longer than the Sistine Chapel."

Mr. Antonelli had also brought religion into our lives.

I don't remember exactly how the subject came up. Maybe I had asked him about the delicate silver crucifix on the chain around his neck. Maybe he had lifted it from its nest framed by the white V of his shirt and held it in his cupped hand for me to see. Maybe I could only think of it connecting their bodies, dangling down between my mother's breasts as he lifted his body over hers. Maybe I don't remember. But he was surprised that our education had not included religion and philosophy.

We searched the library for relevant books and found Aristotle, a dictionary of lives of the saints, a volume on Martin Luther which led to a discussion of heresy, a very old book on the Inquisition in a peeling and leprous red leather cover, and an illustrated pamphlet on demonic possession which Luis claimed for his own. Soon his intricate and angled drawings were peopled with grotesque monsters leering from every corner, creatures with sad and savaged eyes peering over tattered bat wings, as though Luis had all along been waiting to discover who lived with him in his world.

My half-brother and I worked our way through bound volumes of *The Pearl* and other classics of Victorian eroticism and writings of the Marquis de Sade, devouring cover to cover every salacious treatise on the top shelf during our "literature hour" when we were left alone in the breathless vacuum of the sun porch. Tuesday and Thursday afternoons we began a rather haphazard, self-guided study of religion and philosophy. As far as Luis and I could figure out, the Catholics had all the advantages. They could sin and go to confession and be forgiven and have the sin all wiped away. (Luis's hand in satin between my knees until I could not help but open them and he slid his hand higher.)

I wanted to be a nun but Luis laughed because Mother had told us that we had never been baptized and Mr. Antonelli said that only Catholics could be nuns. Luis said that if I wanted to be saved I had to find my original sin so I could commit it and then ask to be forgiven. The more we read from the books on the top shelf of the library, the more impossible it became to even imagine an original sin. Thoughts of holiness and hunger and *musica* and drawing and sin and Luis's hands and feathers and mouths and breasts and smoke all swam together and drowned and reappeared in my waking mind, in my dreams. I was lost and held tightly to the cello.

Then early in the summer that I turned fourteen (and wouldn't tell anyone that I had wished for salvation when I blew out all the candles with one begging and penitent breath), Uncle David came to visit.

The guestroom was prepared for him and for several days before his arrival Mother began smoking more of the thin cigarettes. Mr. Antonelli often extinguished one that still burned in a crystal ashtray, red at one end from the fire, red at the other where it had stolen the color from her mouth, as he lit the fresh one held between her lips. Wine disappeared from the carafe at dinner like the miracle at the wedding at Cana run backwards.

Uncle David arrived one morning with a fanfare blast of the Jaguar's horn. Mother and Luis and I stood in the front hall, Mother between us as if seeking support, the scent of smoke wreathed around her like mist on the bay. Mr. Antonelli stood at the base of the wide steps. His Roman coin profile was reflected in the antique mirror; his hands were clenched in fists in the pockets of his white jacket. Uncle David banged the doorknocker and Mother opened the door.

It was as though another mirror had appeared, a distorted fun house mirror that was not fun at all. Uncle David was at least ten years older than Mother, much taller, hair darker and straighter than her strawberry curls, but they shared the same features. His voice, when he spoke, was deeper, bolder, but it was her voice. They moved toward each other like marionettes, or novice actors in a badly directed stage play who had not yet found motivation for their blocking. They hugged each other without seeming to touch. Mr. Antonelli cleared his throat as though he were going to begin singing a scale for our music lessons and Uncle David stepped back from Mother.

She introduced Luis who shook hands with his uncle. She introduced me, and Uncle David took my hands in his, kissed them and did not let them go. He looked from Mother to me and back again. "She is you," he said to my mother.

"So you said in your letter," my mother replied, pulling a pack of thin cigarettes from her skirt pocket. Mr. Antonelli was at her side with his silver lighter flaming. Mother leaned in to him, cupping her hand around his holding the fire and looked into his eyes for a second. She inhaled, bending the flame towards her. She exhaled, her mouth the roundest and reddest of O's. A perfect ring of gray smoke, parody of a halo, rose, hovered over her strawberry curls then disappeared in the expectant air. "David, let me introduce Dante Antonelli, the children's tutor." Mr. Antonelli clicked his heels together and nodded his head. He flicked his thumb and extinguished the flame with a silver snap that echoed in the hall.

Uncle David did not extend his hand. He nodded and smiled as though he knew that the tutor was painting Mother's portrait and he was amused. He asked for coffee and Cook served it in the parlor. He made Luis and I promise to play for him after dinner, then insisted on taking us into town in his new car. As we pulled out of the driveway in the shiny Jaguar convertible, Uncle at the wheel, Mother beside him, Luis and I in the tiny back seat, I noticed a flash of light in the attic dormer window, as though the sun had bounced off the mirrored surface of a silver lighter.

Downtown we chased cable cars up and down the hills, listening for the hum of the cables under the street. We bought bags of treats at the Ghirardelli Chocolate factory. We plowed through wraiths of fog as we dashed across the Golden Gate Bridge. Mother began to smile, and we thought maybe we would enjoy having our uncle in the house.

But at dinner it was as though the fog had followed us into the dining room. Uncle David took the seat by Mother's right hand, the seat that had been Mr. Antonelli's. The tutor sat at the foot of the table, his square jaw so tightly clenched that I wondered how he could eat his dinner. We had just begun the soup course when concentric circles disturbed the smooth surface of the water in the goblets and etched themselves in our bowls of soup. The electric lights flickered, then went out. In the jumping shadows cast by the candles on the table, we saw the panic on Mother's face as she whispered, "Earthquake." Uncle David took her hand. Luis gripped my hand under the table. Mr. Antonelli sat alone in near darkness looking as if he wished we would all indeed drop into the earth.

I had experienced these phenomena before and had learned in the sunroom that they were caused by a shifting of rock plates beneath the surface of the earth. But at that moment I knew that this particular quake originated not deep in the earth but in the sudden instability of my world caused by my mother's brother returning to this house where they had grown up, fracturing the illusion of solidity in our lives.

It was just a tremor and the lights were soon back on. Cook continued through dessert as though nothing out of the ordinary had happened in spite of the fact that Uncle David was the only one at the table who had much of an appetite. After dinner we tried a bit of the Vivaldi we had been practicing, but our timing and concentration seemed to have been as disturbed as the soup by the shaking of the earth, and Uncle said that he would listen to more tomorrow. We said goodnight. He shook hands with Luis and kissed me on the cheek. Mother bit her lip and turned away and Mr. Antonelli lit another cigarette for her, her hand beneath his not steadying the flame but making it dance and quiver.

That night there were no waltzing steps in the attic over our heads. Luis stole into my bed and just held me while we listened to the angry voices of our mother and uncle. I imagined that pictures on the walls tilted and panes of glass in the arched window cracked into the crazy angles of Luis's drawings during this, our own tremor. It seemed that one entity we barely recognized fought to the death with itself, one voice ripped in two pitches, one jagged note played on the cello and the violin in terrifying disharmony. We heard sobs that could have come from either image in the mirror they shattered between them. When a door had slammed and silence echoed and hummed in the house with the almost voices of the buried arteries of the cable cars, Luis lifted the curtain of my chestnut hair, kissed my neck and crept back to his room.

The next morning Uncle David was gone. Part of my mother was there, but part of her was missing. At breakfast Mr. Antonelli was in his place by Mother's right hand again, smiling and carrying her cigarettes and his silver lighter. Mother's voice seemed huskier, lower, like Uncle David's. She said that he had been called away on business in the East. She said that Luis was going away. She said that Uncle David was sending him to school in Boston. She said that Luis was going away. She said that Uncle David thought Luis needed a man's influence and she did not seem to notice when Mr. Antonelli clenched his jaw and flared his Roman nostrils in anger. She said that Luis was going away. She said that he would leave on the train tomorrow. She said that Luis was going away. She said that Uncle David thought Luis and I were too close, and when I asked her why he would think such a thing, she left the table, overturning her chair, and went to her room.

Luis left the next day. He carried one suitcase, heavy with books from the top shelf. Robert packed the rest of his things in a steamer trunk that followed on another train. Luis lay with me in my bed that night and there were a million fireflies lighting the room from outside the arched window. We didn't care who heard us crying or who might see us kissing, touching, exploring the places we had not dared to search for in each other.

We wrote letters nearly every day. I think Luis liked the school and he sent amusing stories about his classes and sketches he had drawn of his new friends. I was pleased that he drew rounded shapes as though he had escaped the splinter edges of his monster world, but I wasn't interested in other boys and asked him if he had learned more about original sin. I told him that I had taken the new maid into my bed (there were no fireflies that night) and I had tried to lose myself between her soft breasts that smelled of lavender and vanilla and had tasted myself on her body, trying to imagine what he would have found in me. He wrote back that we had probably committed no sin at all and that we had done nothing new (read the Sappho he had left on the top shelf, he wrote). But I had tired of the books and the puzzles of math that solved no riddles I wanted answered and the drawing of fruit that seemed always rotten. The cello was my only consolation.

I never saw Luis again. We received a call in the middle of the night that he had died at school from encephalitis, a fever of the brain. His body was shipped home on a train. I was not surprised that his brain had burned but only that mine had not yet caught fire. Cook and Robert found a preacher to help bury him, and Mother and I stood in the rain as his casket was lowered into the earth that should have shaken in protest but didn't seem to care. My mother staggered in the mud with a new waltz step to stand at the edge of the grave. I don't think she noticed the ash that fell still glowing from her cigarette into the emptiness.

I stopped playing the cello. If God existed, He had taken Luis away. I would withhold my music. But after a few weeks, sleeping in my brother's too cold bed, I began to hear messages whispered in the cello's voice. I walked barefoot through the dark house to the music room and stood in the doorway, my thighs pressed tightly together. For another moment I would deny them the delicious intimacy of the curved wood. On a small oriental carpet sat a straight-backed chair and an empty music stand. A duet of moonlight and streetlight poured through the open drapes and outlined the body of the cello lying on its side. It waited for me with the swelled hips and graceful waist of an odalisque beckoning from a divan.

One by one I raised the fingers of my left hand to my teeth. I bit and tore the crescents of nail and let them fall to the floor. The pad on each fingertip, the *callosita,* must be free to press into the fingerboard and release pure sound. I walked to the cello and slipped it from its velvet case. I ran my thumb over the scar-like purling raised along the edge of its body, then closed my eyes and caressed the swelling back of the instrument. In my mind I saw the book-matched, flame-kissed maple swollen like a soprano's ribcage before the first exhaled note of song.

I tightened and rosined the bow, bouncing the octagonal bow stick against my palm to test the tension of the hair. I carried the cello and bow to my chair.

I did not need a pitch pipe or concertmaster's A to tune, but matched the perfect A in my head to the cello's highest string. The pitch had remained true and only the lowest string, the C, required adjustment. My cheek rested against the scroll. My thighs relaxed with remembered pressure against the wood, which already seemed so much warmer than the night air.

Bowing close to the bridge, I searched for the wolf note. I had laughed out loud when Mr. Antonelli explained the phenomenon, the stuttering pitch at which my cello seemed to howl. Better cellos, with more resonant bodies, suffered more from wolf notes; mutes or cork could suppress or fight the wolf. But I cherished the stuttering, welcomed the flaw, and now sought first the aberration as though it were an old friend who overlooked my own shortcomings. I welcomed my wolf in the moonlight, and then began to play smooth long tones to which I matched my breath, gradually sweetening them with vibrato.

A single exhaled tone became the "Sarabande" from Bach's *Cello Suite Number Five in C minor,* and the tips of my unpracticed fingers grew tender and wept drops of blood on the fingerboard. At the moment the moon retired behind a cloud and blackened the room, my first tears for Luis began to fall.

Six weeks later Mr. Antonelli left after a night of shouting and the sound of splintering wood and breaking glass. I couldn't hear their angry dance above my head because I had slept in Luis's room, in Luis's bed, since he had left for school. In the morning I found my mother curled up on the floor of her room, her window broken by her fists, her hands cut and bloody (so like the stigmata that I craved), polished kindling that had been a violin smashed against a wall, pegs like black teeth scattered on the rug where she lay. She wouldn't say what had happened. She slept or sat in bed smoking thin cigarettes brought to life by a tarnished silver lighter. She still loved him, I think, because she had broken only the student violin, not the one he treasured and caressed with the scrap of blue velvet.

Within a year she was dead. The doctor said it was a stroke. The same borrowed preacher who had prayed over a Luis he had never known said not to question the ways of God but I didn't because it all had happened with the inexorability of a great quake followed by the breaking of gas lines followed by the burning of the city.

Uncle David came back for Mother's funeral. He bought a house a few blocks away and I went to live with him. When I cleaned out the old house after the final black caress took Mother, I found the unfinished portrait in the attic, crammed under the eaves. It had been slashed with a bloody shard of glass that lay beside it. The body in the picture was my mother's, mature, dark-nippled breasts, crooked Cesarean grin on her belly. But the face was mine, and the hair, chestnut, falling straight and heavy to her waist. I lit it with the silver lighter and burned it in the fireplace with the rest of the books from the top shelf.

Uncle David brushed my hair every night in his study until he was stilled and silenced by a stroke. What a strange word. "Stroke" sounds so gentle, so soft, so caressing. Hard to believe a stroke could kill, or make parts of a body stop moving and parts of a brain stop working like the kind of stroke that happened to my uncle. I think my mother was luckier. Sometimes I can hear the whoosh and pulse of my blood winging through my brain as I sit at night beside his wheelchair and brush my hair or play Vivaldi on my cello or read to him about the lives of the saints. They say certain weaknesses run in families.

Egg Money

Sandra Mae Evans hunkered down a mite further in the hair dryer chair, sliding carefully to keep the Naugahyde from making its embarrassing squeal. Her yellow rayon pants suit slid nicely, easing Sandra Mae's pin curls a more bearable distance from the too hot bubble over her head. From extensive past experience—every other Tuesday afternoon at 2:30, as soon as she could get to Chez Arnelle after her favorite soap opera was over and she had fed the chickens—Sandra Mae knew that complaining about the heat would do no good. As she had told her husband, Alvin, over fish sticks last week, "Arnelle just says, 'Turn down the temperature, then!' And everybody in town knows that those danged heater controls have been busted since God wore short pants."

Sandra Mae had no reason to expect an answer from Alvin. For the last seven years or so of their eleven-year marriage, Alvin had pretty much ignored his wife. Oh, he would occasionally say something like, "Sandy M—" (She had asked him a hundred times not to call her that, but he hadn't responded to that request, either.) "Sandy M, is there store-bought mayonnaise in this tartar sauce? I don't see why you've got to keep those stinky chickens if you won't even use an egg to make some homemade mayonnaise from that recipe my ma gave you."

It was one of those questions that started a projector rolling in Sandra Mae's head, and she could see and hear the scene played out just like movies at the Strand when Alvin had courted her in the balcony. She could almost smell the popcorn and his hair pomade. In the flickery light of her imaginary film, she could stand up to him. She would say, "Alvin, the one time I made that mayonnaise, you hated it. Who can figure out how much a tidge of paprika is? Or a splash of vinegar? And one ingredient was plain smeared out by something your ma dropped on the recipe card." In her head Alvin might be reasonable like her dad would have been and say, "I do remember now, Sandra Mae. Thank you for trying that recipe. This store-bought kind really isn't too bad."

Truth be told, her dad hadn't been very talkative either, but in the three years since his death, Sandra Mae had found herself remembering mostly the good things about him. He had done the best he could raising her after her mom died.

These days Sandra Mae found she couldn't argue with Alvin. She had already wasted too much energy trying. When the words wouldn't come out of her mouth, she played mental movies of what she might have said instead of really getting angry with him. She knew if she got mad, he would slam the back door and head out for the garage. She would hear the pickup engine rev and the clutch pop and the worn tires slide on the gravel, and then silence. The house would be as quiet as the broken cuckoo clock, and she would wait up all night for him to come home. Or he would sit on the kitchen chair with his elbows on his knees and his head bent down and his big eyes gazing up and look at her with that James-Dean-sad-puppy expression she had fallen in love with. She would follow him up the stairs to the bedroom to stop the misery she had caused him, both of them hugging the wall on the way because Alvin hadn't gotten around to putting in the banister.

On those occasions that Alvin did say more than, "You better talk to that butcher about how stringy this roast is," Sandra Mae would answer him politely, chatting on for so long that someone passing along the road, a neighbor boy and his dog, or a traveling Fuller Brush salesman, might look through the screen and think to himself that there was a happy couple having a pleasant conversation over dinner, and he would no doubt hurry a little faster to get home to his own loved ones. But if that boy or salesman had happened to glance into the kitchen when Alvin asked, as he did with annoying regularity, "How much egg money you take in this week?" the passerby might be startled as Sandra Mae gazed out the window and into his eyes. He might be put off by a brittleness in her eyes, brown and flat as river stones. He would most likely pull his jacket tighter around his shoulders and he would pick up his pace to move away from the yellow light that spilled through the screen like the yolk of a dropped egg. He might not hear the hardness in her voice that matched the flint in her eyes as she said, "Hen's aren't laying real good right now." It was clear that Alvin hadn't heard her, either.

Her dad had been the one who heard that flint and knew where it came from. He had feared and admired it in Sandra Mae's mother. He was mostly just scared for his daughter when he heard it in her voice one night after she turned eighteen.

Sandra Mae had just come in from seeing *Rebel Without a Cause* for the fifth time with Alvin. He was her very own James Dean. Her girlfriends said he was a dead ringer for the actor they all pined for. The movie had been over for two hours and they had been parked on the bluff talking in Alvin's Chevy. This time they had actually been talking, not making out, the way most of their dates ended. Sandra Mae figured she would rather die than tell her dad that she might be pregnant, but she had told Alvin. He slammed the car door and Sandra Mae could hear his loafers kicking up pine needles a few feet away. When he got back into the car, he didn't look at her, just jingled the keys that hung from the ignition. "You want to get rid of it?"

When she didn't answer, he glanced up. Maybe he felt the flint then. "We could get married."

"I would like that. I'll tell my dad."

Her dad had been waiting up for her as he always did, dozing in his Lazy Boy with a half-read newspaper spread over his lap. Usually she would kiss him on the cheek and say goodnight as she ran up the stairs to her room. This night she sat on the rocking chair that had been her mother's and waited for him to fold his paper and lay it on the floor. "Alvin and I want to get married."

She knew it wasn't entirely a surprise to him. It was near the end of senior year and lots of her friends were getting engaged. But she and her dad had talked about her going to college, starting at the two-year school nearby. He brushed his hand through thinning hair and tapped his upper lip with his pointer finger.

"Sandra Mae, Alvin is a very likable guy but I think this is a decision you need to take more time with."

"Daddy—"

"I'm afraid Alvin is just a starter, honey."

Sandra Mae knew what that meant. Uncle Stanley, her dad's own brother had been just a starter. He had worked in insurance and Fuller Brush door-to-door sales and lemon tree farming in Missouri and breeding chinchillas. Every new project would bring Uncle Stanley and Aunt Helen passing through for a visit. Uncle Stanley would cook a meal in one amazing pot or tout his latest oil well scheme and offer to let her father invest some money and share in the millions they were sure to make. Aunt Helen became thinner and wobblier with each trip, spending more and more time in the kitchen with a bottle of cooking sherry that disappeared with magical rapidity.

"Alvin's practically been promised a job with the radio station downtown. And with his looks, it might not be long before the TV people would pick him up and we could be living in Chicago."

Her dad started to remind her about Uncle Stanley's brief career in show business performing feats of prestidigitation at Ernie's Nite Club on Route 8, but he looked at the daughter he loved, who reminded him of all the good things and the scary things about the wife he missed, and he was quiet.

"Daddy, we want to get married real soon."

Exactly a month later, on Sandra Mae's last night as an unmarried woman, her dad sat her down again in the rocking chair and handed her an envelope with a check for ten thousand dollars.

"This is from your mom's insurance. It's made some interest since then. I know she would like you to use it for your education, but you're a grown-up woman and you can decide where it goes."

The next day he escorted her down the aisle, walking slightly behind her to avoid crushing the hoop skirt of her wedding gown that barely fit between the pews on either side, and he gave his only child away to Alvin.

A few weeks after their four-day honeymoon in the Poconos, Sandra Mae's belated period blossomed crimson on the sheets of their bed. They had lashed together twin beds from Alvin's old room and moved them into an apartment over his dad's appliance store. In Sandra Mae's mind the bed, or beds, tied together but forever knocking into each other and sliding apart with the vigor of their love-making and Alvin's constant tossing and turning, represented their married life. Alvin didn't seem too upset by the news that there was no baby in their immediate future. He liked married life. He could request whatever he wanted for meals and Sandra Mae was willing to try to cook it for him. Where his mom had gotten tired of picking up his dirty clothes and told him to go ahead and live like a pig if he wanted to, his new wife made the dirty clothes disappear and clean ones show up folded in his dresser drawer. She was always there in his bed at night, and in the morning, too, if he woke up feeling frisky.

Sandra Mae, however, realized early on that she had been looking forward to taking care of a baby with James Dean curls and big brown eyes. She puttered around the apartment as she dreamed of a little house with a nursery. The days grew longer and more boring in spite of the black and white TV her father-in-law had given them. Traded in for a Zenith with stereo sound, the hand-me-down set pulled in game shows and soap operas with the help of tin foil flags on its rabbit ears.

One night at dinner while Walter Cronkite droned on about world events, Sandra Mae set a catsup-and-cheese-topped meatloaf in front of Alvin and sidled up to a subject that had been on her mind for weeks. "Alvin, honey, I noticed that the Super Shopper is hiring another checkout girl for the afternoons. I thought it might help out if I applied for the job and brought in a little extra money."

Alvin slammed his fists down so hard on either side of his dinner plate that the meat loaf jumped and the pat of margarine slid right off the mashed potatoes. "Sandy M, I support this family. No wife of mine is going to head off down the street to weigh giblets for old man McGruder and have every bastard in town thinking that things are going poorly up here. You can get that notion out of your head right now."

Sandra Mae felt her stubbornness coming on, but she knew she needed to go easy around Alvin on this one. "Your mom helps out in the store showing how the washers work; maybe I could do some of the paperwork. You know I was always good in math. It's so nice of them to let us have this place and the TV and all. I'd like to help out so they know how much we appreciate it." And that was how, by the next weekend, Sandra Mae became the store bookkeeper.

Alvin's radio career hadn't worked out. He got fired after two weeks when they found out about his reading problems. All it took was a near-riot caused by his announcing a sale on convertibles for two hundred dollars, instead of the two thousand listed in his radio script, and one old man's heart attack, suffered when Alvin misread the farm report and made it sound like the bottom had dropped out of hog and soy bean futures. Things hadn't gone much better with selling insurance or flooring, although they did accumulate a collection of carpet remnants in the basement. Whenever money got really tight, Alvin worked for his father delivering appliances or did handyman jobs around town. Sandra Mae's dad had been right, of course, about Alvin and the just-a-starter problem, but until the day he died, he never said, "I told you so."

Three days after their sixth anniversary, Alvin clomped up the stairs at dinner time, sat down in his place at the gingham covered table, and said, "Sandy M, please come away from that stove for a minute. We have something to discuss." She wiped her hands on the matching gingham apron she had made and sat across the little table from him.

"I know you probably think I forgot our anniversary," he began, "and maybe I did. But it was because I've had my mind full of the perfect plan to insure our future."

Sandra Mae glanced over his shoulder half expecting to see the ghost of Uncle Stanley mocking her. She imagined she could hear the rattle of bottles behind her as the spirit of Aunt Helen rummaged in the cupboard for the sticky sweet anesthesia of cooking sherry. "Just what is that plan, Alvin?"

He pulled out his wallet and laid a business card on the table. EVANS CONSTRUCTION COMPANY / NEW HOMES AND REBUILDS / NO PROJECT TO BIG OR SMALL / ALVIN EVANS III, OWNER, BUILDER. Sandra Mae didn't think to point out the grammar error as there seemed to be much more significant problems with Alvin's plan. "Your dad's name is Gerald," she said, mentioning the smaller issue first. "How did you get to be the third?"

"It sounds more dependable, like the company has been around for a long time."

"Alvin, you don't know anything about construction work." Sandra Mae watched the misunderstood-hurt-puppy look come into those James Dean eyes. "But I suppose if you started with the rebuilds you'd get some on-the-job experience."

"Sandra Mae, that is exactly my plan! Jeb Hazelton is willing to sell us the farmhouse on his land and two acres around it. We'll live in it while I fix it up and you can make curtains and stuff on your mom's sewing machine and we'll sell it for two or three times what we spent on it. Then Jeb will sell us another parcel—that's what the developers call it—and we'll build another house. There you have the start to Evans Country Estates. Won't be long before we have a whole little community built up there."

Damn you, Uncle Stanley, Sandra Mae thought as though her deceased uncle had whispered the scheme directly into her husband's ear. "And just how much startup money would we need for this project?"

Alvin held the saltshaker in his right hand and the pepper in his left and waltzed them together over the checked surface of the table. "I reckon eight thousand would do it for the house purchase and building materials."

Sandra Mae pushed back her chair and returned to the stove. She turned the gas back on under the burner and stirred the macaroni that had turned into congealed pudding. Eighty-five hundred dollars and twenty-seven cents was the amount left from her parents' gift to her. She had never talked about the money with Alvin, had used some of it for the dentist, and to pay the emergency room when Alvin had gotten a fishhook stuck in his hand. The bankbook wasn't exactly hidden; it sat inside the jewelry box in her underwear drawer. But she had always thought of it as a passenger on a leaky boat might view the only life jacket, and felt panicked to know that the captain might have plans for it.

Alvin stopped the dance of the condiments and brought the dented shakers together in the parody of a kiss. "It could be a great place to raise a family."

Sandra Mae's heart hurt at the thought. The flint in her eyes softened and she felt the return of a hope she had not acknowledged for years. Maybe a new start in a real house would be what she needed to get pregnant. "I think we could find that much."

"Jeb said he'd throw in his pickup and camper shell." Alvin went to the refrigerator for catsup to put on his macaroni and cheese and sat back down to wait for Sandra Mae to put his dinner on the table. He didn't ask where the money might come from.

Two months later in the middle of June on the first sticky day of a summer that broke fifty-year heat records, Alvin drove Sandra Mae to the house. The pickup bounced over jaw-jarring ruts through fields yellow-green with new sweet corn. On the door of the truck Sandra Mae had neatly stenciled EVANS CONSTRUCTION CO in paint that had hardly dripped at all. "Shut your eyes, now, Sandy M," he said when they got closer to the house.

"Dear sweet Jesus," was all she could say after he had helped her out of the cab of the truck and told her to look.

"It does have potential, doesn't it." Sandra Mae was glad Alvin had uttered that as a statement, and not as a question she might be required to answer. He reached behind the passenger seat and handed her a magazine. "This is for you, too." It was a copy of *Home Crafts and Décor*. On the cover a woman and young girl posed in the living room of a neat tract house, their identical mother/daughter dresses matching the curtains and slipcovers right down to the rickrack that trimmed all of them. "The first thing we have to do is fix up a place for your sewing room."

Sandra Mae stared at the improbable structure. The original building, a two-story century old farmhouse, had been painted mustard yellow. From one side protruded a squarish addition with a flat roof. On the other side an added on garage had been turned into some sort of room with mismatched windows. Connected to that was another small building that ran into one of the farm's original outbuildings. In front of the whole strange compound stretched a slab of concrete, cracks crisscrossing the surface like varicose veins on Aunt Helen's ankles. Sandra Mae thought of her eight thousand dollars and wanted to cry or beat

Alvin to death with the rolled up crafts magazine. Then she thought of a home for the family she dreamed about. "No, Alvin," she said, marching with purpose toward the front door. "The first thing we need to do is see if the plumbing works and—" She slapped at a horsefly on her elbow. "And find screens for these windows."

Inside, the house was clean but baffling in its odd layout. One unfinished room led to another, each space feeling skeletal as though the couple paraded through the ribcage of a fallen behemoth. Wires snaked in and out of insulation webs. "See," Alvin commented, "Jeb already got started on the remodel work." As they walked together up the stairs, Sandra Mae leaned on the banister. With a crack it gave way and Alvin grabbed her before she could tumble over the edge. "There's a few things need to be tended to," he said. Sandra Mae noticed that not one room had all its walls and ceiling intact. They inspected the two rooms and a bathroom on the second floor and found that the plumbing did indeed work.

Alvin went back for the second truckload of boxes and furniture. Before Sandra Mae began to unpack, she walked the back yard, scouting for a place to hang a tire swing and a sunny spot for vegetables.

The house never progressed much further. Alvin would ask Jeb to come over every few weeks to help with the dry wall or to panel part of a room, and they would end up throwing their fishing gear in the truck and heading off for the rest of the day. Sandra Mae finished the screens herself. Alvin let her paint and hang some wallpaper where the walls were even enough and put down pieces of the carpet remnants. But he came home one day after she had gotten out the sawhorses and wood saw and done a respectable job of putting up a pegboard wall in the kitchen, and he yelled at her that he was the construction person and she had no right to take over his job. He looked at her with his sad puppy eyes, and she looked at the wall with its fresh white paint and neat hooks holding her pots and pans and big spoons, and she realized that Alvin's expression looked pretty silly on the mangy old dog that he was turning into. She put his tools away and went back to doing the paperwork at the appliance store most mornings and watching her soap operas in the afternoon. Some of what she earned went for groceries, the rest was recorded in a bankbook hidden in a far safer place than her underwear drawer.

After they had lived in the house for two years and Sandra Mae's periods had announced with depressing regularity that no baby was on the way, she made an appointment with Dr. Francis for a checkup. She drove to his office in the truck whose door now read PLUMBING AND ODD JOBS squeezed in Alvin's childish printing under EVANS CONSTRUCTION CO. The crotchety, silver-haired physician had delivered and tended to most of the folks in town, and he declared Sandra Mae in excellent health, although she seemed a mite nervous. Was she drinking too much coffee?

"So there's nothing wrong with me?" she had asked.

"Of course not." He tamped down the end of an unfiltered cigarette on his desk. "Out with it. What's the problem, child?"

"Alvin and I have been married for eight years and I haven't gotten pregnant yet."

Dr. Frances reached for a silver lighter on his desk, lit the cigarette, pulled a prodigious quantity of smoke into his lungs and exhaled a neatly divided plume from his nose without taking his eyes from hers. "Alvin never told you."

For the second time in her life, Sandra Mae confronted a question she was glad had been phrased as a statement requiring no response on her part.

"This is a little awkward," he said, waving the smoke away with a surprisingly delicate gesture, "but since you are his wife you have a right to know. Alvin had mumps when he was about fourteen. I told Alvin and his mother then that he would probably be sterile."

Sandra Mae was so quiet that Dr. Frances thought she might not understand.

"I told them that he probably would not be able to father children."

"But there's a chance?"

"It's never a sure thing. I wouldn't want to rely on it for family planning, but after eight years . . ." His voice trailed off like the dissipating smoke.

"Thank you, doctor." Sandra Mae stood and shook his hand. She left his office, then turned around and reentered the waiting room. She picked up a magazine she had been reading, searched through it, and tore out a tiny ad. "Get your degree at home," it said. "Correspondence school. Accounting—" She had read no further. Her first payment was in the mail the following day and was as big a secret as the bankbook.

When Alvin pulled up at the front door with the next sure moneymaking project, Sandra Mae cried with joy. "We live on a farm, right?" he had asked. "Maybe we just need to farm it." He lifted three lambs, a piglet and a cage of peeping baby chicks out of the truck bed. For the rest of the day Sandra Mae hummed and they built pens and spread hay in the outbuilding. Then the pig died and Sandra Mae found his pink body, belly bloated, half buried in the straw. The lambs moved around on legs as shaky as Aunt Helen's; their teary, red-rimmed eyes panicked Sandra Mae because she could not make them better. She arrived home one day from the appliance store and the lambs were gone. Alvin's now battered truck was in the yard and she ran inside the house to find him.

Before she could ask, he said, "The butcher bought 'em. You ought to be glad they were good for something. He's coming for the chickens tomorrow."

"No, he's not." The flint was back and Alvin knew that she meant you will have to kill me to get them, or I will kill you to keep you away. The peeps had been Alvin's best purchase, glossy Rhode Island Reds, one a cock who woke Sandra Mae with his joyous cry at dawn and the rest hens who produced broods of fuzzy chicks and baskets of brown eggs. The chickens stayed and she named each one.

Now, just days short of her eleventh anniversary, Sandra Mae reached her hand under the dryer bonnet, burned her finger on a hot hairpin and clicked off the dryer just as the only other customer in Chez Arnelle left the shop. The brass bell over the door was still jingling when Sandra Mae asked, "Arnelle, what does that sign in the front window say about a manicure?"

"Sandra Mae, you have never ever had your nails done in my shop. You always say those flashing red things would scare your chickens." Then, maybe, she caught sight of the flint. "Why, it's just two dollars with the purchase of your hairdo."

"I would like to have my nails done," Sandra Mae said. She knew there were no more chickens to scare. Saying goodbye that morning to each one, she had let the butcher cart away the offspring with a promise to kill them quickly. He had been surprisingly tender, assuring her that they were meant to be food and she shouldn't worry about them. Their bright colors blurred in her tears as she watched him smooth their feathers, soothing them, as he slipped them into their cages. How wonderful it would be, she thought, to be touched like that. After he paid her and pulled his truck away, she called the original six and they came to her like pet dogs, or obedient trusting children. One by one she snapped their necks and watched as their attentive eyes turned to jet-black beads. She had boiled them in a pot on the stove, plucked their rainbow feathers and dressed them for the freezer.

"Well, you just pull those pins out of your hair and let me set up here, and we'll give you a manicure while your curls cool down."

It was funny that they were still friends. A year ago Arnelle had just broken down and cried, tears dripping into the bowl of perm solution she was dabbing on Sandra Mae's head. "I didn't mean to sleep with Alvin," she had sobbed. "But he was just there. He's the best handyman in town and the sink was really broken."

"That's OK." Of course it wasn't OK, but Sandra Mae had told her cousin in Dubuque months before that she thought Alvin was cheating on her. It was better to know the truth. Maybe Alvin was sleeping with every woman in town who had plumbing problems. Sandra Mae had blotted at the drips of evil-smelling liquid threatening to overrun her eyebrows while Arnelle swore that she would never see Alvin again, and Sandra Mae found herself in the odd position of trying to stop Arnelle's tears. In her soap opera, there would have been someone to comfort her, the wronged wife.

Sandra Mae laid the hairpins on the worn but clean white towel that Arnelle had draped over the manicure table and wheeled in front of her client's chair. Without a word, she lifted Sandra Mae's hands so the fingertips with their short and savaged nails hung limply in warm water. If she noticed that Sandra Mae's wedding ring was gone except for a thin, untanned stripe of skin encircling her ring finger like a half-exorcised ghost, she didn't mention it.

On her way to Arnelle's, Sandra Mae had made her first and last visit to the town's only pawnshop. She knew from crumpled tickets in Alvin's pockets, and the disappearance of things around the house, that her husband must be quite well known there. Inside the tin-roofed building dim light had filtered through the dust on the front window etching Barlow Pawn—Jewelry and Firearms in fuzzy letters on the floor. The last two words seemed whispered; someone had scraped at them with a razor blade until only the outlines remained.

She had glanced around the shop, gripping her purse close to her chest. The room seemed a cross between an antique store and a prison. An asylum orchestra of dented, abused musical instruments slouched in corners and hung like undiscovered suicides from hooks in the ceiling. Small kitchen appliances waited expectantly on shelves, toaster ovens with mouths agape, plastic radios longing to sing Top Ten again. Against the wall facing the front door stretched a counter topped by bars and chicken wire. Below the counter, watches, bracelets, brooches, and rings lay on shelves behind glass. Sandra Mae had moved closer to the counter as though she might better hear their sad stories.

A man appeared behind a gate in the fence over the counter and Sandra Mae jumped, jarring a suspended tenor sax that swung her distorted reflection back and forth. He was shorter than Sandra Mae by several inches. He had brushed strands of his silver hair carefully over the thinning crown and the sweet deception reminded her of her dad's only vanity. "How can I help you today, Miss?" Her tears had probably surprised her more than it did this witness to everyone's hard times.

She took out a tissue and searched inside her coin purse for the ring she had taken off that morning after she killed the chickens. She laid it on the counter. "How much can you give me for this?"

The man opened the little door to the cage he was in, pulled a jeweler's loop from his pocket and squinted it into his right eye. As he picked up the ring he asked softly, as though he hadn't played this scene a thousand times, "Are you sure it's over between you two?"

She nodded. The tears were gone and the flint was back in her eyes.

"I can't give you more than thirty-five dollars for it."

Sandra Mae nodded again. She held out her hand and the pawnbroker counted out the sum in wrinkled fives and ones. She had hurried out of the shop and walked two blocks to Chez Arnelle.

Now Arnelle leaned to the counter beside her chair and turned on the pink plastic radio. A broken-hearted, three-times-wronged cowboy gave up on his cheatin' girl and went to bed with his bottle of whiskey while Arnelle pushed cuticle and tried to give some shape to Sandra Mae's sad nails. As each nail was finished, Sandra Mae whispered, "Thank you," under the guitar's twang and the cowboy's nasal complaints.

When she had finished the sixth nail, the pinky finger on Sandra Mae's left hand, Arnelle sighed. "I know you never had a manicure before, but for gosh sakes you don't have to thank me after every nail. You can just say thanks at the end if you want."

"I'm not thankin' you. I'm thankin' Faith and Hope and Charity and Lucy and Ethel and Little Peeps." With each name, Sandra Mae tapped a newly respectable fingertip on the towel. "My egg money's going to buy me this manicure." And there would be plenty left over for a new life in her own little apartment. Nearly a thousand dollars was wrapped in oilcloth and stuffed in the feed bin, more than enough for a lawyer and a train ticket to Dubuque. Her cousin said the packing plant was hiring for the night shift, and if Sandra Mae had to start on the assembly line she knew she could do that. But at the bottom of her packed bag at home lay her accounting diploma and the promise of a better job than her cousin's. Sandra Mae's daddy had taught her to plan for a rainy day, and storm clouds had been gathering on the horizon for some time now. "You have room in your freezer for some fryers? I could bring you a couple tomorrow afternoon, plucked and dressed."

"Why that would be really great. This manicure is on the house. What color polish do you want for your nails?"

Sandra Mae pointed to "Hidden Passions," a crimson as bright and shiny as the feathers of her Rhode Island Reds.

Girls Climbing Trees

The last time I went home—to settle my father's estate, clean out the house and put it on the market—I noticed that the oak tree that had been planted on the day I was born now stretched skyward above the house like the hand of an excited first-grader begging to answer some long-forgotten question. The summer that I was sixteen, the strongest limb brushed fingers against my second-floor bedroom window. The whisper of leaves against the glass blended in my dreams with the imagined caresses of older boys, boys who were the heroes of my fantasies, stars of my diaried scenarios. Ten years later, whispered rumors and articles in the local paper would chronicle the fall of many of them to jail sentences, failed marriages and barroom brawls. Robby, who lived next door and taught me to climb the tree, turned out to be the only true hero and died in Nam. But sixteen doesn't know.

My best friend, Cecelia, was an only child like me. The difference between us (in addition to the fact that Cecelia had long honey-colored curls and my straight brown hair usually hung in a lifeless ponytail down my back, and the fact that she had a figure that drew whistles from the time she was in seventh grade while I was, in my mother's words, willowy) lay in the fact that my parents seemed to have a life separate from my existence and Cecelia's didn't. I was always secretly grateful that they had spared me the pressure Cecelia must have felt to live her parents' lives for them. My mother's days revolved around teaching second grade; nights were filled with grading blue-lined manila papers and cutting up construction paper for craft projects. My father was always available for homework consultations and rides to football games, but if asked, would identify himself as an independent insurance agent and offer to give you a free quote on auto coverage. Even if they hadn't been asked, my best friend's parents would announce that they were Cecelia's mom and dad, Cecelia who had been named for the patron saint of music, Cecelia of lessons in ballet and voice and piano.

The very end of summer meant the arrival of boys at the university just a few blocks from our house. Fraternity parties gave Greek letters the mystique of incantations that might transmute us from girls into women—and Cecelia had been invited. She revealed her plan to me as we walked home on a Friday afternoon, she from her dance class, me from my babysitting job.

"We've got to sneak out tonight and meet at the corner at 11:30." Cecelia tossed her blond curls out of the way and lit one of the cigarettes she carried in a tampon holder in her purse.

"Your parents will kill you if they find out," I said. I wasn't sure what my parents would do. I had thought about sneaking out ever since Robby showed me how to search for footholds and move up and down the limbs that laddered from my window to the ground. It had seemed like a good possibility to keep in mind should any Nancy Drew-type mysteries ever come my way.

"Just meet me. I'm going to wear my new miniskirt. Can I borrow your white halter-top?" My mother definitely frowned on lending or borrowing clothes—or anything else. But Cecelia was my best friend.

"Sure. Come on over now and get it."

Because it was a Friday night, I knew my parents wouldn't bother me until Saturday noon. To this day I can sleep in late if given the opportunity, although that deep dead oblivion of adolescent slumber has long eluded me. But if I had inherited my mother's sense of adventure, the eagerness to explore the unknown trail, I had also been endowed with my father's caution. I couldn't ignore the possibility that they might come into my room and, finding me missing, assume the Lindberg-baby worst. So after I dressed in new jeans and my second-favorite top, I left what I hoped was a reassuring note on my pillow and climbed down the tree.

Cecelia was waiting. Even though she stood in the shadow of wisteria bushes, her hair glowed in the streetlight's reflection. A wisp of smoke from her cigarette made her look like the heroine from a '40's detective movie. We headed quickly toward the university as quietly as our giggles allowed.

Noise and music announced the party from a block away. A banner emblazoned with TKE hung limply from the center balcony of a two-story brick house. Through the windows silhouettes jerked and bobbed to the frenzied beat of a talentless but passionate band screaming out "Hang on, Sloopy." Candles flickered, blue lights and strobes distorted the space inside. Half a dozen guys stood around with bottles of beer or paper cups in their hands. This leering welcoming committee eagerly opened the door for us.

"Cool." I could smell alcohol on Cecelia's breath as she leaned over to whisper into my ear. She had bragged about stealing from her parents' liquor cabinet but I'm not sure I believed her before that night. She headed carefully across the crowded floor that was already slippery with spilled drinks. Perched in the middle of a long table was a porcelain toilet holding a punch bowl. A very unsteady young man poured bottles of grain alcohol into the bowl and mixed the concoction with pitchers of what looked like cherry Kool Aid. With the exaggerated care of the inebriated, he ladled the liquid into a paper cup and handed it to Cecelia. Before he could fill a cup for me, I spotted and claimed the last Coke left standing amid the dropped potato chips and pretzel remnants littering the bed sheet-draped table.

Cecelia reached into her purse for a cigarette and three boys reached out to hold her drink for her. Cecelia slipped the cigarette between her lips and half a dozen lighters added their flickers to the room's unsteady illumination. Cecelia paused, looking into the eyes of each light bearer in turn, then reached out her tiny hand (which could barely reach an octave at the piano, she had often mentioned) and cupped a huge hand (which seemed bred to catch footballs) as if to steady it. She leaned toward the chosen one, touched the fire with the tip of her cigarette and inhaled; even the flame bowed in her direction. Cool, I thought. She followed as he shouldered open a space for them on the dance floor.

One of the runners-up in the competition for Cecelia asked me to dance and we joined the masses that thrashed about like palsied marionettes to "Louie, Louie." Partners changed and I found myself slow dancing with a skinny young man who confessed to being a poet as we clung together to the tribal beat of "The Lion Sleeps Tonight." We found an empty spot on the stairs to the second floor and I let him spike my Coke with Jim Beam from the flask he carried. He read his poetry to me from folded sheets of lined notebook paper. Neither the heat of passion nor the judgment-clouding effects of the alcohol were enough to convince me that the poetry was even passable. It simply reminded me that I had a headache, it was getting very late, and I hadn't seen Cecelia for at least half an hour.

I excused myself, and before I had finished muttering some kind words about his sonnet, he had turned away to find a more appreciative audience.

It took me about ten tries to find someone who had seen Cecelia. A marginally coherent girl in a half-unbuttoned blouse nodded toward the stairs and said, "Try Tim's room." The band had quit or passed out and music from a stereo thumped through the building as loud as the band had been, but in tune.

The hallway upstairs was dimly lit by the spill of light from partially open bedroom doors. Fetid wet heat generated by the late August night and too many bodies made me feel that I had stepped into the gut of a sick animal, like Jonah in the belly of a beached and rotting whale. A girl moaned and vomited in the bathroom. I called Cecelia's name. A male voice said, "Across the hall."

I tapped on the door across the hall. Something inside dropped to the floor. A bottle? A body? A slurred male voice shouted from inside, "Stay the fuck out of here." I turned the handle and barreled into the room as I imagined my father might have done as a young Marine at Normandy.

The room was even gloomier than the hall had been. It smelled of sweat and sex and beer and the mellow ghost scent of marijuana. A fat candle burned on a saucer beside a mattress on the floor. Flickering light reflected off the tangle of Cecelia's golden hair. I thought she might be dead. The man she had danced off with knelt over her, swearing at, fumbling with, his belt buckle. I rushed at him, pummeling him with my fists. Without even aiming, he threw me to the floor with a backhanded blow. I fell hard on my side. An empty bottle rolled from where my arm had hit. Colt 45 Malt Liquor. The big bottle.

I stood up, grabbed the bottle by the neck, and whispering, "Oh, Jesus," swung it as hard as I could against the back of his head. I took a step away from him because it didn't look like I had stopped him at all, just diverted his attention. He stood up and looked at me, through me. He had lost interest in his belt buckle. He seemed to be almost smiling when he toppled forward, not even stretching out his arms to cushion the fall. It was too dark to tell whether the wet streaks in his hair were sweat or beer or blood, and I truly didn't care.

Cecelia was breathing. The halter-top that she had borrowed lay torn on the floor, but I didn't want to hang around long enough to find something to cover her with. I managed to half carry, half drag her to the door. In the hall the poet stood, shirt unbuttoned, supporting a girl with eyes raccooned by mascara. She gagged and turned quickly back into the bathroom.

"Christ," he said when he saw Cecelia. He took off his shirt and handed it to me but didn't meet my eyes. He went into the bathroom and closed the door.

I managed to get Cecelia down the stairs and out to the sidewalk. There was a slight breeze blowing, some real air to breathe, and she managed to stand on her own. Clutching the shirt closed with her tiny trembling hands, she looked no older than she had as the third-grader who invited me to her house for cookies the first day she moved to town. "I have to call your parents," I said. There was a pay phone at the end of the block. My father always insisted that I wear penny loafers with dimes in them for emergency phone calls.

She started to cry as we reached the phone booth. "You can't call them. I'm so ashamed. I can sneak back inside and they'll never know." She was sobbing, and I gave in. With the first dime I called information, with the second I called a cab. While we waited, I held her hair back as she vomited into the grass. Her hair no longer reflected the moonlight.

"Is she all right?" the driver asked. He sounded genuinely concerned.

"I think she'll be fine," I said, giving him Cecelia's address. "But I only have two dollars."

"Don't worry about it."

The cab was silent except for Cecelia's hiccoughed sobs.

As we pulled up to her house, I saw all the lights on. The front door was open, Cecelia's father's slump-shouldered silhouette hung like an expectant ghost against the screen door. Before the cab had stopped completely, he was out the door and striding toward us, bathrobe flapping, peeling bills from a roll of money to pay the driver.

"Forget it," the driver said through the open window. "I got three daughters at home myself."

Cecelia's father helped her out of the cab and into the house where her mother's shadow now loomed in the doorway. Like the writer of bad sonnets, her father had not met my eyes either.

"Can I give you a lift home, Miss?"

"No, thank you. I'm just two houses away." Without the cab to announce my arrival, I still had a chance of getting back in undetected.

The Nancy Drew part of me knew that I should stick to the shadows in the yards on the way home, but the scared part of me knew that I had seen enough darkness to last many nights. There were no lights on in the house, but I felt as though it, too, had been waiting up for me. I climbed back up the tree and fell into my bed. I cried myself to sleep.

For the next week I raced to retrieve the morning paper. I expected each day to read about a violent death in the fraternity house. It even sounded like the crime in a Nancy Drew mystery, but one that she would have been expected to solve, not commit. I dreaded seeing a police artist sketch of me, my father's eyes, my mother's nose, my own limp ponytail. But there was no word.

There was also no word from Cecelia. When I finally called her house, her mother told me that Cecelia was concentrating on practicing the piano and would not have time to see me. School started and her father drove her to school and back home again. It was the first time we hadn't walked together since we met in third grade. When she turned seventeen, I was the only one of our crowd not invited to the party.

A few weeks after school began, I walked home alone to find that my tree had changed. The limb that brushed my window was gone. Only the full moon of the tree's wound and a sad pile of sawdust were left. My mother would only say that they had waited far too long to prune the oak. It was dangerous to the house for a branch to grow so close, and I knew that was true.

I always meant to ask my parents if they knew about the late night adventure, but I never did. Now both of them are gone. I had forgotten about the whole event until my daughter was born. "Forget the silver spoon," I told my husband. "Just plant an oak tree for her."

Tracker

Carolee watches most intently the ones who have not come to mourn her son. Since calling hours began, she has not allowed her hand to lose touch with either the polished oak edge of Ben's coffin or the cool satin of the lining or the colder softness of his hand. She moves around the coffin as though it were the last piece of wreckage left floating after some terrible tragedy at sea, knowing that it will not support her weight, yet afraid to lose contact with it. If she believed more in its security, she might climb on top and wait for rescue.

Carolee's fingers trail across the satin as she moves closer to the head of the coffin. Her eyes scan the room for David, her younger son. Before she can find him, she sees the reporter from Detroit who interviewed her this morning. Carolee remembers the reporter's name, Nancy Martin, and recalls that she seemed gentle and sympathetic. But she had been there to interview them and she was a newspaper reporter and she must be there looking for a story.

Nancy catches Carolee's eye and nods, but Carolee wonders if Nancy is really looking past her at Ben, looking beyond the slightly bemused expression on his face, imagining headlines that might run above her byline. "Bloody Tracks in Snow Lead to Questions," "Hunting Accident? Local Police Investigate." Carolee takes a step to her right, placing herself between the reporter and Ben as though she might shield her older son from nodding a subtle clue to the mystery.

Nancy has turned to speak to a tall man. He has approached with his face averted from the coffin, but now as he pauses beside the reporter, Carolee digs her fingernails into the glossy finish on the coffin's wooden edge, scratching a signature of panic. She had not recognized the chief of police out of uniform. She is surprised at how at ease he seems in his dark suit. She wonders if he is wearing a gun, in a shoulder holster, perhaps. She thinks that if he is armed, his tailor has draped the pinstriped wool extremely well.

Carolee tries to guess what Nancy is saying to the chief. She can't remember his name and wishes again that Arthur Bluesett hadn't retired a few months ago. Arthur had been best friends with Carolee's father. They had hunted together since they were boys in Gobles, just a few miles from Kalamazoo. Kids in Gobles still got a day off from school when hunting season started. Arthur understood accidents.

Watching Nancy gives her no clues to the conversation.

Carolee reaches out with her free hand to grasp the hand that Barb Evans thrusts towards her. "I'm so sorry," Barb says, squeezing Carolee's fingers. Barb had been Ben's English teacher his senior year at Kalamazoo Central. She had threatened to give him a failing grade for cheating on his final exam, but Carolee's husband, Chuck, who teaches phys ed at the same school, convinced her to change her mind. He has always been good at getting women to change their minds.

Barb leans so close that Carolee can see dark roots in her butter-blonde hair and can smell the cheap vanilla-musky perfume she wears, perfume Carolee has smelled on Chuck's pillow. She drags the perfume down into her lungs like a junkie starved for an opiate cloud, wishing a screen between her and the sickly odor of formaldehyde that clings to Ben. "Are there really reporters here from the *Free Press*?" Barb seems as surprised as Carolee by her question. Always the diplomat, Carolee's instinct is to defuse the awkward moment, but she looks into Barb's eyes for the first time and enjoys her discomfort. Barb drops her hand and moves away, muttering another "Sorry."

The reporter had called early that morning and requested an interview. When Carolee hesitated, Nancy asked her to think about it and call her within an hour at the Holiday Inn if she was willing to talk.

David was sitting at the kitchen table. He dropped his coffee cup when the phone rang but the cup hadn't broken that time, just splashed a last swallow of cold coffee on the cherry-stained pine table. "Do you want to call her back and tell her we're too upset to talk?" he asked.

Carolee watched as David laid a paper napkin on the liquid and stared at the brown continents forming on its surface. She wished she could look into his eyes for an answer to the best way to deal with the reporter. He did not meet her gaze, had not looked directly at her since he headed off for the hunting trip with Chuck and Ben three days earlier. Carolee feared that he had made the last decision of which he was capable as he nodded to her and left through the kitchen door, shouldering his twelve-gauge shotgun and whistling for Tracker. The old hound had followed the three of them out into the snow.

"No." Carolee needed to start making decisions. "I think we should talk to her." She began dialing the number she had written down when the reporter called.

Within fifteen minutes, a dark blue Jeep Cherokee had driven up the driveway and Nancy was knocking at the door. David had not moved from the table except to refill his coffee cup. He sat hunched over it, close enough for the steam from the hot liquid to fog his thick eyeglasses, only nodding to acknowledge his introduction to the reporter. Carolee and Nancy sat a few feet away in worn matching overstuffed chairs that Carolee had covered with hunter green corduroy years before.

As Nancy began what must have been her standard speech about how sorry she was to intrude on their sorrow, making it sound spontaneous and sincere, Carolee was aware that the reporter's gaze was taking in the room, the closed shell-curve of David's back, the clutter of photographs on the bookshelf. Suddenly Nancy stood and crossed to the oak bookcase. As Nancy passed her, Carolee caught the scent of soap and a trace of cigarette smoke, too transparent to mark her as a regular smoker. She wondered if the reporter, on assignment, alone in a motel, had allowed herself one cigarette, on the balcony, perhaps, furtively waving the smoke away in denial even to herself of her secret vice. Or had it been like the lipstick smears or the tracks of manicured nails that Chuck had brought to her bed, unaware, clues left by careless lovers.

Nancy focused on a large framed picture on the middle of the top shelf and picked it up. "Is this Ben?" she asked, the professional respect in her voice not quite masking the genuine curiosity underneath. She studied the photograph of the boy, who appeared to be about fifteen, and the man who stood with his arm draped around the boy's shoulder. Except for the difference in height and body mass, and the slight suggestion of gray in the man's hair visible below their matching hunting caps, they could have been twins. Both stared at the camera with glacier blue eyes and triumphant, amused smiles.

She concentrated on the rest of the photograph. Against a backdrop of dull sienna and ochre of late autumn woods, the hunters in camouflage posed over the gray bulk of a fallen five-point buck. The deer's head had been tilted up as though it studied its killers, searching for motive; it rested against the forest-mottled thighs of the older man. The boy stood with one foot on the buck's flank in a parody of the "great white hunter" stance. Their expressions suggested that only the photographer had grasped the irony. Blood streaked the cheeks of the boy, bathed the hands of the father, pooled wetly in the buck's wound.

"Is this Ben?" Nancy asked again.

"Yes."

"It's a good picture. Who took it?"

Tortoise-like, David swiveled his head to look at her for the first time since she had entered the room. "I did. I shot them both that day." He looked at her with eyes the same dark brown as his mother's, as if daring the reporter to draw any conclusions from his remark.

Carolee held her breath for a second, afraid that the reporter might sense a hardness in her son, the dark edge of those killer instincts so obvious to Carolee in David's father and brother in the photograph. She prayed that the reporter saw only a young man tormenting himself with guilt over the accident.

"It was taken when Ben was just fifteen, eight years ago." Carolee had jumped in quickly. "Would you like coffee?"

"Please. Black." Still holding the hunting picture, Nancy looked at the rest of the photographs as Carolee moved to the counter to pour two cups of coffee, touching her son's shoulder as she passed him. David pulled further into himself, tightening the inward spiral away from them. Most of the photographs were of the dead son: Ben wearing a football helmet, cradling a trophy while he was carried on teammates' shoulders, Ben surrounded by adoring cheerleaders, Ben in a letter sweater speaking from a Rotary Club podium.

"And you were how old?" Nancy asked.

A man's voice behind her answered, "Fourteen," and Carolee wondered how long Chuck had been listening before he and Tina entered the room. She saw recognition and mild shock on Nancy's face as the reporter identified him as the man in the photograph and saw that he looked twenty years older. He could have been father and grandfather to the hunters. An old, sway-backed hound followed them into the room, sniffed at Nancy's loafers and lay down at David's feet.

Carolee handed a mug of coffee to Nancy and introduced her husband, Chuck. He reached out to shake hands but never moved from the young woman's side. She had copper-colored hair that reached her shoulders. Her hands were thrust deep in the pockets of a black cardigan that she held close together in front of her pregnant belly like curtains closed on the set of a play not quite ready for opening night. Her face might have been pretty but was red and swollen from crying, her eyes so puffy they seemed slanted. She suddenly noticed the photo in

Nancy's hand and ran from the room into a hall leading toward the back of the house. The older man turned and followed her, calling, "Tina." They disappeared down the hall. A door closed.

"That was Tina." Carolee suddenly sounded exhausted, barely able to exhale the name.

"Ben's widow?" Nancy laid the picture down and reached for her tablet and pencil.

For a second the only sound was the clicking of a ring against a china mug. "My wife," David whispered.

The dog at his feet churned his short legs in a dream chase, growled deep in his throat and released a fart that smelled like death. David didn't seem to notice. Carolee gave an embarrassed smile and shrugged her shoulders. "That's Tracker. Now you've met the family."

Carolee had expected the *Free Press* to send a tough investigative reporter. She knew the police report and stories in the local paper had raised unanswered questions. Why were no marks found at the place where the gun was fired if David had slipped in the light snow, accidentally discharging the rifle, as he had claimed? Why had Ben turned to face his brother, taking a bullet in the heart? Why had David been following so far behind his father and brother and the dog when the accident occurred? Suddenly the reporter seemed not to care about pursuing the story. Did she want to leave them to their grief? Was she eager to get back to Detroit to follow up on a more important story? Carolee felt both relieved and vaguely insulted.

Nancy put the notebook and pencil in her purse and said goodbye to David who nodded toward his coffee cup in response. She expressed her sympathy to Carolee as they walked to the Jeep, and promised to attend the viewing that afternoon. As Nancy pulled out of the driveway, Carolee turned and stared for a minute at Tina, framed in a window, hands still clasped in front of her.

In the subdued light of the funeral parlor Carolee looks down at her right hand and sees that her clenched fingers have massed the coffin lining to a damp, wrinkled ball. As she smoothes it she realizes that Tina has moved silently into place beside her at the coffin. Carolee does not acknowledge her daughter-in-law. Out of the corner of her eye, she watches the curve of Tina's pregnant belly as it moves in time with her sobs like a shaken new moon. The old Tina is back, Carolee thinks, the timid, quiet mouse that David brought home two years ago, his first girlfriend.

They had both attended Western Michigan University. David and Tina had studied at the house afternoons and evenings, and Ben had been home from Michigan State more and more weekends. They had practically become a threesome, a foursome, Carolee thought, if you included Chuck. And Tina had "blossomed" (Chuck's word); she had blossomed under the attentions of the three men. There was laughter and electricity at the dinner table. Several nights a week they crowded into the TV room to share popcorn and beer, and watch videos of movies or old high school football games that Chuck had coached and Ben had won for the team.

When she had to pass through the room to the kitchen late at night to fill the coffeemaker, Carolee tried not to read the configuration of bodies awake and asleep on the floor and sofa. She had given up offering to drive Tina back to the dorm. When David had more studying to do, Chuck would take care of it. He didn't want Carolee to have to go out late at night. She was sure she could smell the scent of Tina's perfume on all of them.

The funeral director smells like mothballs and mouthwash. He comes close to Carolee and whispers that the casket must be closed in five minutes. Carolee feels like the air has been knocked out of her and she doesn't answer. She is concave, hollow, as empty of life as Tina is full of new life. She fears that she can no longer remember the blue of her first son's eyes, the son in whom she found endearing the magnetism she now despises in his father.

Chuck reaches the casket and, even with Tina between them, Carolee catches the reek of whiskey on him. She will not meet his eyes, can live without a reminder of their blue. The smell of Wild Turkey knocks her back to late night four or five months ago when she found David drunk in the kitchen.

She didn't know if it was David's sobs that had wakened her. Ben and Chuck had gone hunting.

Carolee had fixed a cup of coffee and sat across the table from David. His tears turned to rage and he paced the kitchen floor. Carolee waited. Finally, as a hint of sun began to silhouette pines outside the window, David sat with her at the table. "Tina's pregnant."

Carolee took a swallow of cold coffee. She knew that on at least two occasions Chuck had slipped Ben cash for "taking care of things" with girlfriends. She had stopped wondering how much of their own savings had gone into similar problems that Chuck had created. "What are you going to do?" she had asked. "Do you want to marry her?" She had not thought to ask what Tina might want.

David had held the whiskey bottle to the light, tilting it so the amber liquid pooled in one corner. With exquisite care he had unscrewed the cap and poured the drink into his glass. He held the bottle upended, staring at the last drop as it swung slightly. "I don't even think it's my baby." He had said it so quietly she had leaned closer to hear him. She smelled the alcohol and the sweat-soaked cotton of his flannel shirt and the ghost of a casserole she had heated up for their dinner.

"Whose baby do you think it is?"

The bottle smashed against the inside of the porcelain sink but neither of them flinched from the arc of glass shards. "You know who." David's voice was even fainter, as though he were being choked. And she did know, was sure the answer had been in their house forever, the answer that smelled like Tina's baby-powder sweetness and Barb's vanilla musk and dozens of other women's scents, stenches.

"What are you going to do?"

David's fury had broken with the bottle. "I'm going to marry her." He headed for his room. "And then I'm going to kill him."

He had turned back to her, waiting for a response, waiting for his mother to jump up and slap him, to scream that such a thing was inconceivable, to wash his mouth with soap, to treat him like an impossible six-year-old. But she had nodded ever so slightly, as though preoccupied. She might have been acknowledging a muttered announcement that he was going to put the trashcans at the curb. David had gone to his bedroom. Carolee had reached into a closet for the broom and dustpan.

Carolee smells the camphor calling card of the funeral director before he appears at her side. Tina has stepped back to stand beside David. As Chuck moves closer to Carolee, she sees that his eyes are as glazed, as dead as those of the buck in the hunting photograph. The parade of colognes that changed with his women has been replaced by an emanation of rot and whiskey and loss. At the funeral director's nod they grasp the edge of the coffin lid to close it. Chuck's and Carolee's hands touch and both seem slightly startled, but it has been a meaningless accident as when their bodies touch in bed and they pull quickly apart.

Carolee glances around the room. The new sheriff has left. Nancy Martin crosses the room to offer final words of sympathy and Carolee is relieved to see that Nancy seems quite perfunctory, bored. The reporter has none of the bird-dog intensity Carolee feared at the start of her morning visit.

Barb Evans joins the family at the closed casket and asks Tina about the child she is expecting. "Do you have any names picked out?"

Before Tina can reply, David grasps Tina's bent arm and answers Barb's question. "If it's a boy, we're going to name him Ben. After his—" He pauses. It is an intentional, pointed, surgically precise incision, a breath-held gash spilling a story to which he will never again allude. "Uncle."

Revival Meeting

It was my cousin Sue Ann's idea to sneak out and go to the tent meeting. I told her and told her that my daddy had made me promise not to leave the house until he and Aunt Hattie got back from taking Momma to the hospital. Sue Ann said don't worry. She was almost fourteen and I was just ten and my daddy (her Uncle Samuel) had put her in charge and told me to listen to her.

"It's practically like going to church, Nona," she said to me. Her words came out kind of scrunched because she was holding her lips still and putting on the lipstick she wasn't supposed to have. "It's not like it's a dirty picture show or something. Why wouldn't your daddy want you going to church?"

Now that was a sore subject in our family and Sue Ann knew I didn't want to talk about it. Momma was an every Sunday member of the Church of the Brethren. She wore her long hair wrapped in a bun covered by a prayer cap. She read her *Upper Room* magazine of devotionals every single night before she went to bed. As far as I could tell, she had only done one thing in her whole life that the neighbors could gossip about over the back fence. My momma fell in love with and married my daddy, the best car mechanic in town and a fallen-away Catholic who hadn't been inside a church since the day he married her. I knew—and Sue Ann knew—that he would call the tent meeting kin to the carnival that came through town every fall and Momma would say, "Samuel, that's blasphemous." Then there would be words, hard words.

I told Sue Ann the lipstick made her look just like Sandra Dee and I picked up Momma's old purse that I had taken to carrying wherever I went. When I opened the clasp that looked like real gold, I could smell lavender talcum powder and peppermint and it felt like Momma was right there and would go along to the tent meeting. We headed to Frye's field, leaving the old box radio playing softly to fool burglars who might come by. That was my daddy's idea. He grew up in the middle of Philadelphia, and even though nobody around here even locked their front doors, he always said, "Better safe than sorry." Seemed like he had a saying for everything.

A huge crowd had already gathered at the field still stubbled with the whiskers of last year's cornstalks. July's tardy sunset glowed through the open windows of a school bus. Hand-painted letters on its dented side proclaimed "East Hanover Baptist Church—Jesus Reins." Folks had come from all over.

As soon as Sue Ann and I filed into the tent, moving as careful as tightrope walkers on the canvas covering the rutted field, I knew why she had left her *Top Fifty Hits* show on WKPA and her new movie magazine to go to the tent meeting. Henry Woods, red hair flaming, grabbed Sue Ann's hand, leaned her against one of the stout poles holding up the tent and began nuzzling her neck like they were all alone instead of in the middle of half the town gathered for Jesus. Henry was the son of a preacher and a real hell raiser. Sue Ann giggled him off and sat me down in one of the folding wooden chairs near the back of the tent. The chairs were stenciled with "Blaughman's Funeral Home" on the back and fat women all around me waved egg-shaped cardboard fans courtesy of the same sad business.

Sue Ann told me to hold tight to my purse and stay right where she had sat me and she would be back in a jiffy. Then she and Henry slipped through the canvas panels that had been left untied. I started to worry about where she was going and what I would do if she didn't come back and what if she let Henry do unspeakable things to her and she became a fallen woman. Sue Ann had been letting me in on some of the facts of life. Our mothers were sisters, and Sue Ann had overheard them talking about the hospital visit. Sue Ann told me it was about woman troubles. She also told me that if a boy put some of his parts close to some of your parts that's how you made a baby. I just couldn't believe that my momma would do that especially with her prayer cap and devotionals beside the bed at night. What Sue Ann described seemed like an awful lot of bother and I wouldn't wish it on Momma even if I wanted a sister more than anything, which I did.

I forgot all about the state of my cousin's soul and Momma's woman troubles when the Reverend Benjamin Sotillo stepped on to the stage.

He was more handsome than the movie stars in Sue Ann's magazines. Bobby Darren, Eddy Fisher, James Dean—who could compare? There was no doubting that the preacher was a man of God. Mist rose up from behind the stage and floated around his feet. His black hair was slicked back from his brow. His dark eyes swept the crowd and I knew he had seen into my soul. I don't remember a word of his sermon. A heavenly choir, maybe Methodists from Lancaster, sang hymns behind him. Women everywhere in the tent stopped fanning, laid their hands on chubby thighs and leaned forward to be closer to him. From behind the canvas came the sound of tambourines. A snaky trail of sweaty farmers and their wives shook and shouted toward the stage and Reverend Ben thanked God for the spirits filling the people and letting them speak in olden tongues from the Bible.

Reverend Ben was crying now. He had pulled off his suit coat. His soft white shirt was open at the throat and sweat anointed the hair on his chest like holy oil. He asked for the afflicted to join him on the stage and I tried frantically to think of something that might be wrong with me, something the touch of his hands could cure. A man in a flannel shirt, far too hot for July, swung across the stage on crutches. The preacher laid his hands on the cripple's uneven shoulders and the man tossed his crutches away, dancing with joy to the applause of the crowd. I thought of my left arm, broken the summer before in a fall from the hawthorn tree, but it had healed straight as ever with Doc Baker's plaster cast. A blind man was led on to the platform, was smacked on the forehead with the reverend's palms, and threw his dark glasses to the floor, smashing them with his boot. I hadn't even had a cavity since I lost the last of my baby teeth.

Then I remembered Momma in the hospital and I was ashamed that I hadn't thought to pray for her. I waved my hands in the air with the others and promised God that if he healed her woman troubles I would go to church every Sunday and give my lunch money to the poor and listen to my father's sayings and—become a nun. I knew Reverend Ben wasn't a Catholic, but surely he would be impressed at the next tent meeting if I had given my whole entire life to God.

There was a commotion at the main flap of the tent and a poor creature with filthy, tangled hair and tattered clothing came tearing down the aisle, growling and slobbering like a mad dog. Reverend Ben whipped off his belt and snapped it in the air pleading, "Jesus, this man is possessed of an evil spirit! Cleanse him!" Just as the man/animal leaped at the preacher and the crowd rose to its feet, the preacher braced himself, feet apart, and demanded in a terrible low voice, "Get thee behind me, Satan." He had whispered it, really. But no one in the crowded tent had missed the message, least of all the demon in the man. He dropped to the ground, Goliath felled by David's stone. He flopped around like a puppet with its strings all tangled. He curled up in a ball. Then he stood up, mad no longer, and hugged the reverend like a brother. The crowd went wild with Praisethe-Lords and Alleluias, and the man without the demon in him began to pass the collection plate.

Reverend Ben told us about millions of children starving in China because the rice crop was bad, and all these farmers turned their overall pockets inside out, placing sweaty, folded bills into the brass plate with hardly a second thought for their bad crops and their own sick kids. I looked into Momma's old purse and found the two nickels my daddy made me carry for emergency phone calls or milk money. I dropped them in with careful, exaggerated moves as if they might be silver dollars or gold pieces. Mrs. Bradley, the librarian, slipped her wedding band off and dropped it in with a muffled clink. She didn't even watch it disappear under the pile of dollars. She just stared at the man of God and he stared back at her.

Pretty soon the Methodists, or whoever the choir was, started to sing "Rock of Ages" and the crowd dribbled out the main flap of the tent, glancing around to be sure there were no more demon-maddened men outside. The Reverend Benjamin Sotillo glided through the flaps behind the stage and Mrs. Bradley followed him a few minutes later, not even bothering to look around to see if anyone she knew was watching.

True to her word, Sue Ann showed up before the tent was empty. Her blouse was buttoned up crooked and her Sandra Dee lipstick was gone, but she looked happy. Henry Woods walked us home.

We got to the house just as Daddy and Aunt Hattie pulled up in the car. The radio was still playing inside and no burglars had showed up. When we explained that we'd gone to the revival meeting to pray for Momma, and Henry had escorted us home for safety, Daddy said, "A stitch in time saves nine." I couldn't figure out what that had to do with anything, but at least he didn't yell.

They said that Momma had to stay at the hospital for a few days and in a couple of months she was going to have a baby. I let out a "Halleluiah" and wished I could speak in tongues. God is surely good, I thought, waving my arms in the air like the ladies at Reverend Ben's tent meeting.

The very next week I went to the five-and-dime and bought a string of pearls. Sue Ann said that Catholics prayed with beads to keep track of their prayers, and I wanted to get started on my nun work right away.

Momma stayed in bed a lot and I helped out around the house. Everything seemed to be going fine until about five months later. I had turned eleven by then. I woke up in the dark when Momma screamed and I heard Daddy cry,

"Holy Mary, Mother of God," and I ran into their bedroom. Momma's face was as white as candle wax. Between her spread knees I saw my last and only chance for a sister, still and bluish, connected by a cord to Momma. The quilt was red under them like the baby had been wrapped in rose petals inside my momma's belly. My daddy shooed me out of the room and told me to call Doc Baker. The red had smeared on his hands and pajamas and I knew it was blood from woman troubles.

Momma lived. She asked me if I wanted to name the baby before they buried her but I couldn't tell them that I would always think of her as Rose, and so the headstone just said Little Girl Brewster.

After that my daddy never mentioned Holy Mary or God again, and he seemed all out of sayings. Momma didn't go to church so much. She cut her hair short. I don't know what happened to her prayer cap. I broke the string of pearls and threw them one by one into the ravine near our house. The shiny part was peeling off and I was starting to suspect that they weren't real pearls after all.

Red Letters, Gilt Edges

(After Flannery O'Connor)

(She lay there, eyes closed, wriggling her hips deeper into the straw, securely tucked into the familiar warmth and smells of the barn. He was beside her, had to be beside her, had promised to stay beside her.)

The man had wandered up the road only hours ago. Elegant somehow, silvered with dust, carrying a huge and equally dusty Bible under his arm, he had asked if she were the lady of the house. Ignoring the limp, the clumping across the porch, his eyes never wavering from hers, never dropping to the hated limb, he had asked if she were the lady. And she had—without a second thought, with hardly a second thought that her father and brothers were in the field and her mother in town—she had answered, "Yes," and backed as quietly as she could to the wicker porch sofa.

He didn't seem to notice the awkward maneuvering required to force the leg to a wooden sit or how it jutted unnaturally from beneath her skirt and petticoat. His eyes gazed comfortably, unembarrassed, into hers. Gracefully he sat beside her, lending her an unaccustomed grace. He opened the Bible across their laps. The man, her visitor, talked of family pages, gilt edges, and red letters for what Jesus spoke, as he wiped the dust away, grazing her hand.

(He was so quiet beside her now. She didn't want to think that he was too quiet and held her breath to better hear his sleeping sounds.)

He had talked on. Talking over her, until he said, "Proverbs and Psalms are my favorites. Because of the poetry. Do you have a favorite book?"

He had to ask her a second time before she answered. And then she had answered only indirectly as her mind flew off. She took a deep breath and whispered the words she had never thought to speak out loud. "I write poems." He hadn't caught the words and leaned closer. She took an even deeper breath, inhaling with the warm air the scent and hint of the taste of him, sweat and dust spicing a faint bay rum. He leaned against the lifeless leg casually, unoffended, as though it were as fleshed as any lady's leg. "I write poems."

"Let me read them."

"No one has ever read them."

He smiled. He smiled at her. "You must have read them."

"I'm no one."

"Then let me be the first."

(She knew now that he was no longer in the loft, no longer beside her. She almost giggled, thinking that he had probably sneaked down the ladder to relieve himself behind the barn, and would soon be back beside her. She thought of her brothers running down the steps on cold mornings, peeing like horses on the grass rather than dashing to the outhouse.)

"I keep them in a secret place."

"Then take me there. Show me the secret place."

Thinking back, she knew that she had realized even then that he meant to see more than the poems. But no one had asked before. And no one was likely to ask again.

She carefully laid the Bible aside. "Come with me to the barn." He held out his arm to her as gallant to lady, not crutch to cripple. And she took it as a lady. Their walk to the barn was ever so slow. He paused every few feet to comment on a hovering bird or the neat hedge or an exotic cloud, as though his interest in the surroundings, and not her halting gait, necessitated such a leisurely pace. He hesitated just inside the barn door, seeing her move toward the wooden ladder stretching to the hayloft.

"You can climb that?"

"Yes, slowly," she answered, smiling. "But they don't know."

(Lying there, her eyes still tightly closed, she admitted to herself that he was not in the loft, was not just outside, was not returning. Refusing to think further, she thought back.)

"Then I'll follow you." He had followed, so close behind her, she wondered if the ladder would hold the weight of both. She climbed, half pulling herself up the wooden poles, no longer afraid of splinters, eager to reach the top. She glanced back and froze in shame at the sight of his head half-canopied by her ballooning skirts. "You're beautiful," he said, his voice slightly muffled. "Keep climbing." And she had, pulling herself over the top rung and flopping into the hay.

His eyes, nose, mouth appeared a second later as he joined her in the loft. "No!" He had tried to stop her from rearranging her skirt over her legs, the real and the one she thought of as "the other." "No. I want to look at you." But she had turned over and half-stood, crouching under the sloping ceiling.

"I want to show you my poems."

"Of course." Had there been a hint of impatience in his voice? "Let me read a poem." She had pulled out the cigar box tied shut with a Christmas bow and brushed the straw away. Carefully opening the box, she chose a spring poem, a lighter one. If he understood, the painful ones would follow, and be shared at last.

He read it. Quickly, she thought. "It's beautiful." He folded the poem and put it in his coat pocket. Had she told him he could keep it? No matter. "You're beautiful," he said, taking off his coat and draping it carefully over the single ladder rung visible at the loft's edge. "Lie back."

She had. She didn't know why, really. Because maybe he could read that fast, and understood her pain, even from a lighter poem. Because—maybe "just because." Maybe, she thought, because a poet, an artist, is supposed to experience life. And this had never happened before. And would never happen again.

She opened her eyes for the first time since waking, and stared straight up at the beams. A sluggish, egg-fat spider spit out a web close to her, connecting a rough beam to the small round loft window that grayed the light it grudgingly admitted to the secret place. Her eyes searched the web and its seemingly more substantial shadow for some break in the natural pattern, some acknowledgment that the spider had glanced down and, seeing their love activity below, had recorded it by deviating from its pre-ordained design. But the spider, unimpressed, had continued to spit out an any-spider web, scrambling off the pattern just to wrap a dinner fly.

She had lain back in the straw and let him undress her. She had let him look at her, at places no one had ever seen, places she had denied existed except when her monthly cycle forced her attention there. Even then, she tended her body as she would have the wounds of a friend, distant, objective, denying disgust. But she had watched him watching her, had allowed herself to share his pleasure, and then had let herself find her own joy in the skills of his hands and mouth.

When he entered her, she took pleasure in the pain, because it was such a little pain to one who had known so much.

Her eyes wandered now from the web to her body, slightly surprised at the still red tracery of blood on one thigh and the almost copper stain on the straw below. She sucked in air as the sight of blood brought to mind—as it always did—the memory of that day. The one they never talked about. She had been ten years old, hiding from her dad, playing a secret game in the fields. Listening for the tractor, standing up suddenly in the field, seeing her father's face above the wheel, knowing he was too close to turn, hearing his one shriek—and falling into blackness. Where was the blackness now?

She shifted to gaze out the window, making no move to wipe away the crimson marks, careful to avoid the web. She almost laughed at the sight of her "other" leg leaning at a jaunty angle against the trunk of the pear tree below. The tears began when she noticed a white scrap of poem crumpled beneath the wooden foot. She dropped back, blinking away tears to read the shadow of the spider web. Fragile clock, the shadow had shifted with the sun's fall. It must be nearly four and her father would be back soon.

As if in confirmation, the cows, udders full, complaining softly, moved restlessly below. For the first time, she noticed that the top rung of the ladder no longer broke the loft horizon. She crawled to the edge and looked down to where pushed blades of straw drifted through the dusty air. The ladder rested on the barn floor. How carefully, how stealthily he must have placed it there. An accidental fall would have wakened her. He hadn't liked good-byes. Beside the ladder, a pitchfork poked rusty spikes into the air. Daddy will be furious with Tom, she thought. He never puts his tools away. She stared at it a while. Had the fork moved slightly? The spikes, four beckoning fingers?

She rolled back from the edge and slid along the loft floor to reach the poem box. Her daddy would be back soon, would see the leg outside, would replace the ladder, would cover her nakedness and her blood with his plaid shirt, would carry her down the ladder across his shoulder as he had carried the yearling calf last winter. And he would say nothing. As he had said nothing about the calf last winter, lost and nearly frozen, carried on his broad shoulder.

She read her poems and, satisfied with them, sorry that one had gotten away, carefully retied the Christmas bow and buried the box under the straw in one corner.

She crawled to the edge again, unaware that the straw and loft floor had marked her with redder stains than the ones now fading on her thigh. Red as the Bible letters for the words that Jesus spoke. She was glad to see that the prongs no longer threatened, but smiled four matched smiles from the barn floor. She pushed herself over the edge, moving freely, gracefully, as she moved only in her dreams. Twisting like a dancer in midair, she fell heart-first on to the smiles of the pitchfork, which pierced her more gently than the man had.

Repossession

Well, what would you say to the nurse who rushed to cover tiny cloven hoofs before she handed you your newborn son? O.K. I admit I wasn't entirely surprised. I guess I didn't let myself think too much about the bad things that might happen and just hoped for the best.

He was the prettiest little thing and fit perfect in the crook of my arm. He stared up at me and smiled, and when I nestled him closer, I swear he winked just like his daddy. The nurse hadn't said a word as she pushed the wheelchair into the hospital room, settled me in it even though I told her I was right as rain and could surely walk out on my own two legs, and handed me the baby. "Excuse me, but does that—" I nodded toward what should have been the toe-end of my baby. "Does that happen a lot?" I just had to ask.

The nurse's velvety blue-black skin seemed even darker against the white of her uniform. She looked at me for a second like she thought about pretending that she didn't have the foggiest notion what I was talking about, but then she winked that same slow wink and said, "It do happen on occasion, Miss."

"Can I talk to the doctor about it?"

"Now what doctor would that be, Miss?" she asked. She seemed friendly and polite but she did come down hard on the "Miss" part like she knew I'd bought my wedding ring at the five and dime on lunch break. The ring had a glass diamond cut like a heart with little squarish red stones on both sides and the saleslady said it was a direct copy of a movie star's ring she saw in *People* magazine. It hadn't started to turn my finger green yet, but I suspected that it might pretty soon.

The nurse's voice had island music in it. The short order cook at Tootin's Biscuit World where I wait tables is from Jamaica, so I figured from her accent she must be from somewhere in the Caribbean, too. "The doctor who delivered my baby."

"Why that'd be Dr. Cul and he's not here anymore." She picked up the chart that had been hanging at the foot of my bed and pointed one very long fingernail at a scribbled signature at the bottom. "Ref I. Cul, M.D."

"Is he Indian?" I asked. The name didn't sound familiar. As she moved the chart away, I felt a chill that shook me clear through. I'd spent two summers working the desk at Sharpe's Motel and had gotten good at reading signatures upside down and backwards as people signed the register. What I saw in Dr. Cul's backwards name made me glad he wasn't around any more. It came to me right then that I didn't remember much of anything about the night before when Josie'd brought me to the clinic on the outskirts of Charleston straight from working the night shift in Pocatalico. Seemed like I'd met a different doc every time I went to the clinic for my checkups, and most every one was a foreigner, but I sure didn't remember any Dr. Cul.

The nurse leaned over to wipe a little drop of spit from the baby's chin. She was laughing to herself and the sound made me hug the baby closer. "Oh, he's not likely from around here." She stood up and tucked a little bag of something hanging on a chain around her neck back inside her nurse's uniform. Now, I hadn't been outside West Virginia in my twenty-six years, but I had heard mention of voodoo and warding off the evil eye and such. That little velvet bag made me think of shriveled up chicken's feet. She let out a little more of that nasty laugh. "But I don't think he's from India. Nope. I never heard it called India."

"So he's gone for good?" By now I mostly just wanted to get out of there and back to the apartment.

"Oh, I reckon he was on call for one of the other doctors. Not likely he'll be back any time soon. Not likely." She put a plastic bag with a tiny bar of soap and a midget tube of toothpaste beside me and hung my purse over the handle of the chair. "What you gonna call this fine young man?"

I hugged my baby a little closer as she pushed us fast down the hall and out the door to where my friend, Josie, waited to drive us home in the only taxi in Pocatalico, West Virginia.

"I haven't quite decided yet." I didn't want to seem rude or anything, but I don't think I'd have told her even if I did know.

As we pulled away, I heard her cackling some more. "His daddy might have some ideas about that. Hell, yes, his daddy might done thought up his name." I turned around in the back seat and looked out the window, but all I saw was a patch of fog like a dirty cotton swab.

I cranked down my window part way and met Josie's eyes in the rear view mirror as she pulled the cab away from the curb. "Looks like you got yourself a fine baby there, Nona. Boy or a girl?" Josie's voice always surprised everybody. She talked in a husky, breathy whisper that sounded for all the world like Marilyn Monroe, which wouldn't have been so weird except that she was built like a Steelers fullback. She was a good woman, though, and had dropped another fare when I'd called her from work the night before when my water broke just before closing. Josie'd made me promise to call her for a free ride home from the hospital.

It didn't seem necessary to say anything at all about his minor foot problem. The powdery clean baby smell in Josie's sometimes-smoky cab made me want to cry with loving him. "Perfect little boy," I said, kissing him smack in the middle of the black curls that pretty much covered up the two little bumps on his head. The very second my cheek touched those nubs, the dream I'd been in for the last nine months stopped like a jackrabbit meeting buckshot. It was like I woke up knowing that I had gotten both the baby and me into an awful fix and I was going to have to figure a way to get us out of it.

Quick as anything, Josie'd driven us down Tupper's Creek Road all the way to Eden's Fork where we lived. She helped us out of the car and up to the side door that went to our apartment at the back of the Meckler's house. "Do you need any help in?" It was nice of her to ask but I could tell she'd as soon pick up a rattlesnake and put it in her hip pocket for the ride back as come into our place. I hadn't realized it before, but there was a bad feeling that leaked out and puddled around the whole block. The sunlight was a dim greasy yellow on the peeling paint of the house. Even the grass looked sickly and the trees drooped. No wonder Josie glanced at the shadows like she couldn't get out of there fast enough. I thanked her again for the rides and said we'd make it fine from here. She disappeared down the Fork, dust and black exhaust from the cab dogging her wheels like a rabid hound.

The apartment was dark and hot. Even when I pushed aside the curtains, the sun didn't seem any more interested than Josie in coming inside. Somewhere squirreled away in the back of my mind was the memory of that very same room full of light and breezes when I lived there all alone. The baby squirmed in my arms. I could feel my milk coming in and I tried to remember what the visiting La Leche lady had told me that morning about feeding the baby. As I sat in Momma's old rocker, I must admit I was kind of scared and real glad it was just me and the baby there. It didn't take long for that hungry little one to figure out how all this was supposed to work. We were both dozing in the chair, rocking lazy, when Eblis came home.

He was wearing the plaid wool cap with a bill that he said was what all the fancy Englishmen wore. Believe it or not, I'd never seen him without that cap, in bed or out. Now I'm not as hollow-brained as you might be thinking, and I blame my lack of curiosity on that dreaminess I was just now breaking out of, but for the first time I started thinking about what kind of curly horns might lie under that wool. He pulled the cap low over his eyes and sashayed cockier than ever over to look at the sleeping baby. He leaned closer than I wanted him to and winked. "Well, ain't that the cutest little devil. What're we going to name him?"

Deep down inside I was thinking about that "we" and not liking the sound of it at all. "I haven't figured that out yet" was all I said, wishing he would just back away and stop breathing on the little thing.

Eblis was prancing back and forth across the floor. Not even the tiny leather boots he got handmade from somewhere really fit him and he'd taken his shoes off as soon as he got inside like he always did. The damn click click clicking was really driving me nuts. "Asmodeus!" he shouted, spinning in the air a couple of times.

"You've got to be kidding," I said. "No teacher at Pocatalico Elementary could even spell it."

He looked disappointed for a second. "Clootie?" I started to say something nasty about that idea, but his black eyebrows were coming together in a dangerous frown. "That was my uncle's name." His voice sounded real low now and with Eblis that was scarier than another guy's shouting. I just shook my head and held the baby closer.

Suddenly I had to look away. He was doing those crazy little dance steps that had gotten me in trouble in the first place. "Beelzebub!!" The name exploded out of him. Sparks flickered around his hairy ankles, drops of spit sparkled on his chin, the curls on his head seemed to squirm like vipers in the pit. "We'll call him 'Bubba' for short and no one will know!"

I guess it was at that very second I knew what I had to do. Eblis laughed so hard he had to lie down and take a nap. While he snored and snorted in the bedroom, I called the cab company and wrapped the baby up good. We waited outside on the stoop. Josie smiled and looked relieved when I told her I needed to go to Our Lady of Sorrows right away. It was clear across town, right beside the Sunbeam bakery, but she wouldn't take a penny for the ride and said to call her if we needed a ride back or anywhere else.

Now I had been raised in and out of a couple of Protestant churches, but it seemed like the Catholic Church was where I ought to go with a problem like this. A nice man in a long black dress met me at the door and told me I could come in and talk to him even if I wasn't a Catholic because he had two hours before the Bingo game started. He told me to call him Father Michael, which seemed a little silly because he wasn't much older than me, but if that's what he wanted me to call him I would. I just took a deep breath and held on to my baby and laid out the whole messy story for him. About how Eblis walked into Tootin's Biscuit World one night with his Englishman's cap on his shiny black curls and sweet-talked me and soon we were dancing to the music on the radio that we only turn on after the customers have gone and we're sweeping up and putting the chairs back where they belong. And how the late shift cook left us alone in there and I woke up the next morning in the back booth knowing I wasn't the same girl who'd walked in ten minutes early for my shift the day before.

While the speaking part of me was going on to Father Michael, the brain part of me was having what my Momma would have called an old-fashioned sit-down talk-to with myself, trying to figure out when the dream had really started. To be honest, it might have started when I was about twelve years old and the choir director told me I had the sweetest voice she'd ever heard, and then it got dreamier when I was fourteen and the cheerleading coach said I kicked higher than those Rockettes out of New York City. My senior year the school paper ran a picture of me in my "Our Town" costume with the headline, "A Star is Born," and reality in Pocatalico lost all its appeal. Now if my Momma had still been with us, I suspect she would have told me to go after that dream, work at it, even if it meant being the first one in our family to leave West Virginia. But she had passed away when I was in eighth grade, so I read movie magazines, tried every new shade of lipstick that came out, and hung around waiting tables at Tootin's Biscuit World hoping to be discovered.

Most every guy in town came into Tootin's at some time or another and every one seemed duller than the one before. There's nothing like watching a man drip red-eye gravy down his chin, or listening to him slurp coffee and belch into the sleeve of a shirt he's worn for a ten-hour shift at the plant, or wiping up the catsup splatters around his plate for a two dime tip, to make a girl think that Prince Charming probably isn't going to be from around here. When Eblis made his tiny-toes, hip-swiveling, plaid-capped entrance into the café near closing time, I should have known that trouble was coming through the door. But I dropped my common sense on the floor and ground it in like a dab of yesterday's mayo. I remember posing in front of the Mr. Coffee machine as he sat down and spun around on the stool a couple of times, stopped with his elbows on the counter, and framed me with his thumbs and pointer fingers like he was seeing me in a fancy picture on the wall. The night shift cook, who wouldn't usually leave me alone with a customer, and a stranger at that, turned on the radio, nodded to Eblis, and left with the floor just half mopped like he was already deep in his own dream.

You're probably dying to know what happened next and what was it like doing the deed with a devil and did he promise me things like power and money, or at least a walk-on part in some miniseries. The truth is I don't recall. I do remember thinking that he must be the handsome stranger who would take me away from here and dress me in beautiful clothes and give me a Hollywood house to live in, and then the memory gets foggier. The next thing I know for sure is he's moving into the tiny apartment I pay for with my salary and tips from Tootin's. I'm late for work every morning because even plain saltines won't stay in my stomach. Then I'm holding this precious bundle and am scared to death for him.

The baby slept, and I told Father Michael about the three-dollar ring I bought when I started showing, and sharing my apartment with Eblis, and how I knew it was my fault 'cause I'd danced with the devil but now I wanted to make it right.

When I looked up at Father Michael, his eyes were shining brighter than Eblis's eyes. He went out of the room for a second and came back with some water in a pint Mason jar. I'd washed about a million of those since I was a little girl, helping with preserves and tomato sauce, but this one seemed special. He held his hands cupped around it like there was a tiny flame inside and he was the only one on earth who could keep it from blowing out in some terrible wind. He asked me what I wanted to call the baby and looked real pleased when I said that Michael seemed like a fine name. He made some signs with his fingers and said words I couldn't understand. I held my breath when he bent down and kissed the top of my baby's head, but when he smoothed out those curls I could tell the little nubbins had completely disappeared. Then he walked us outside to a white van with some dents in the bumper. Peeling red letters on the side said "Tuesday nite BIN O—Cash & Priz s" and the address of Our Lady of Sorrows. He put me and Little Michael in the back seat, wedged the jar of water into the coffee cup holder, and drove us home.

I walked in with the baby, and Father Michael was right behind me. Eblis met us at the door and was already starting to fume and sneer like he smelled something really awful. First thing I said was, "His name is Michael and he's just got baptized" and then I ducked and got out of the way. The whole thing must have knocked Eblis off kilter. He sort of pinged around the room like he was being slapped by flippers in God's pinball machine. Momma's rocking chair flew, books did somersaults off the shelves, curtains shimmied like strippers with arthritis. Finally he did his sparking dance steps backwards and Father Michael pushed him into the front hall closet. I admit I had a moment of weakness when Eblis looked at me with his big dark eyes, his curls shaking under the brim of the plaid cap, and I remembered that he was supposed to be my way out of Pocatalico. But I looked at Little Michael, awake but not afraid in my arms, and knew where the truth was. As soon as the door slammed shut, Father Michael put some holy water on it with his thumb and said "Amen."

When he turned back to me, his face looked a hundred years older over his black dress. He handed me the water jar, whispered "Bless you," kissed Little Michael on the forehead and backed out of the front door. I could barely hear the van drive away over the noise coming from the closet. Such swearing and snorting and gnashing I never hope to hear again. He called on Kali and cursed Kronos and called out to Moloch so loud two pictures fell right off the wall. Greeny-yellow light flashed under the door. I could see bits of a spinning shadow going round and round.

That was three weeks ago. There's hardly a glow under the door any more, no more than what a dying lightning bug would make. And I haven't heard a sound. I stuck a couple of nails in it just in case. I went to see Father Michael yesterday but they said he was on a retreat. That must be like a holy vacation. I just wanted to tell him thank you and let him know that the water he left was doing great on Little Michael. I rub it on every day after his bath, and his toes are growing in straight and pink and perfect. Now if I can just get him to stop winking at me.

Still Life

Emily contemplates her left foot. She is not a young woman much inclined toward contemplation, but now she watches, head slightly tilted, as her foot curls and twitches and bends and stretches quite independent of her will. It is a dancer's foot, narrow, high-arched, the second toe slightly longer than the great toe. It is calloused, abused, depended upon. She slides to the edge of her bed and stands, straightening out the errant foot with the weight of her body. She moves with a dancer's grace even as she winces from the bite of the pin that holds two sections of her hip together.

She is lucky to be alive. Emily repeats the mantra she has heard chanted over and over by her doctors and her mother. On the way to the shower she turns on the radio to a country music station. The songs about cheating lovers and one-night stands help drown out the metronomic pulse that beats constantly in her head, the throbbing count of the practice piano that drove her feet across the wooden floor or through the air. She thinks she might die if she heard Tchaikovsky or Stravinsky.

Turning on the hot water, she watches it swirl into the drain. She sits heavily on the edge of the tub, ignoring the pain in her hip, pressing her hands tightly against her eyes. On the veined and mottled backdrop of her eyelids she sees the spinning lights of her dream the night before. Her sleeping mind has begun to recall the accident.

For the past three months Emily has retained no memory of the event. At the trial she learned that a young man had run a stop sign and struck her car on the driver's side. He sat in the courtroom with his head bowed, looking genuinely remorseful. A certain song had come on the radio, he explained, it was really special to him and his girlfriend, she had just broken up with him, he had to find another song because the first was just too painful, he reached for the radio knob, he didn't see the stop sign, he didn't see her car. Emily thinks it is ironic that her life as a dancer has ended because of teenaged angst, an adolescent broken heart.

Even though she studied the street diagrams the lawyers held up and listened to the details of the accident, the event remains locked in some black cell in her brain. Witnesses testified that her car had spun around several times. She remembers the spinning in her dream and imagines that she must have tried "spotting," a trick ballerinas use to prevent dizziness as they pirouette. Everything after the nightmare spin is still lost in darkness. Her mother says the memory loss is a blessing. Emily is lucky to be alive. Emily steps into the shower.

She tries to lose herself in the steam and too-hot water. She scrubs over the scars as though she can erase them. She ignores her left foot that has curled its toes up like the end of a sultan's slipper.

Emily walks down Market Street toward the San Francisco Bay. The doctors have told her that walking will help strengthen her legs. She avoids walking close to the ballet school where she taught, where through an open window she might hear rehearsal music or the brush of leather-slippered feet whispering *jetés* across the floor. Her grandmother's Kodak camera bounces against her chest. It hangs from a strap of cracked black leather. The man at the camera store was impressed that all the parts still worked and he sold Emily film for it; 35 millimeter, he said. Emily thought it sounded like artillery ammunition.

She pauses at a corner and focuses the camera on the ocean's curve in the distance, but the shape is too close to that of a dancer's arm, rounded, embracing space, and at this distance she can see the movement of waves. She lets the camera fall to her chest and looks for a more static subject.

Emily hears a rattle of coins and notices a man in ragged fatigues crouched near her feet. Out of habit she reaches into the pocket of her jacket for the loose dollar bills she has always carried for the street people. She fingers the paper and thinks that this man is lucky to be alive. He should get up and go look for a job. She pushes the bills deeper into her pocket and walks on.

She steps through a puddle of water on the sidewalk, afraid to jump over it. If you were walking behind her, you might notice the pattern her wet feet make on the bricks. For ten steps it is a perfect herringbone created by her dancer's turnout. On the eleventh step, you notice that her left foot has flopped a bit to center, then she slows as it careens even further toward the right foot, muscles contracting uncontrollably. You might not notice the tears in her eyes or hear her stifled sob as you turn quickly up a side street, Powell perhaps or Kearny, going out of your way by a block or two to avoid her awkwardness.

Emily takes several photographs as she wanders along the dock. She is not interested in the skateboarders or in-line skaters who fly past her. She will not admit to herself that she is envious of the blur they would engrave on the film. Emily is pleased with the complicated pattern made by a construction fence over an iron balustrade shadowed on a wall. She focuses on a leaf, then drops the camera, a jerked weight around her neck, when the wind lifts the leaf, allows it a dance. She frames only those things most stable, those totally devoid of movement through space. She thinks that perhaps she might work on a collection of still life photographs, a menagerie of the inanimate. As she walks back to her apartment, Emily decides that "still life" is an oxymoron, a contradiction. Life is movement; life is dance.

It is nearly dark when Emily arrives back in her apartment. She raises the parchment folds of her blinds, collapsing them like the bellows of a silenced accordion. Whatever glow remains in the sky from the setting sun is smothered by the shroud of fog that has rolled in from the bay. She unties the laces of the clumsy supportive shoes she has worn since the accident and throws them under the bed. Emily sits in her overstuffed chair and lifts her feet to the ottoman, unaware of the grace of her movements. As she leans to massage the calf of her right leg, the camera bounces in her lap, its leather strap still around her neck. There is one shot left. Emily, lucky to be alive, aims the camera at her left foot and clicks the shutter, just before her muscles clench and bend the foot into a most unnatural curve, like the neck of a dying swan.

Atavanna, the Risen

My sister's arm dangles between my thighs like a tentacled penis. An opposable thumb and four crabbed digits scratch arcs in my flesh with ragged claws. The Keepers do not acknowledge her existence. They say I have scratched myself. They mummy my hands with scrofulous bandages, gauze surreptitiously unwound from the dead.

Don't look at me! Lower your eyes. So few still recognize the honors due royalty. We have ignored the niceties, civilities and courtesies until they skitter into corners, catch in spider webs, and sway there, vital juices sucked dry. Even if I let you look, you would say you didn't see her—just as the doctors claim not to see her, the Keepers refuse to acknowledge her, even our mother, weeping, denies this desiccated husk of a sister leeching and bobbing from my body.

On pain of death, you dare not say a word against my mother. For all her blindness she is still the Queen. But I am fifteen and ripening, and soon I shall ascend the throne.

My parasitic, putrefying sister is fifteen and withering like a wormy poisoned apple in the witch's hand. I call her now Xanaxia, the Feeble. If they admitted that they saw her, they would call us conjoined twins, but I prefer the quainter designation "Siamese." If I let you look at me, you would see that I look Siamese, exotic. Remember Elizabeth Taylor's Cleopatra eyes? She copied them from mine, kohl-rimmed tilted almonds. I used to stain my sleepy lids with the very same pencil, the one Liz gave me, the one I sharpened to a pointed end of pain, the one the Keeper ran into with her shit-brown eye, the one she drove into the weak mush of her brain. The pencil they took away from me. Keepers are so clumsy and so stupid.

My mother does admit that mine was not a single birth. She says that there were two babies, but claims them separate. I was the first-born princess, crying hosannas in mystical harmonic chords never heard on earth. She was limp and still stillborn, neck corded, cords umbilical and bloody wrapped around her scrawny neck, around my chubby fists. Now she is borne and I bear her, wear her flopping at my side.

We share one heart. They will deny it but I hear them whisper that her blood, once red, is rusting now. Mine turns ever-purer blue. I find hers dripping down my thighs sometimes. She is weakening.

I do not allow her to eat any more. It is easy to pretend that she has fallen asleep when the flimsy stalk of her neck bobs and droops and plops her witless head on the table. They do not see her pale eyes pleading, her fish mouth opening and closing soundlessly. I used to feed her. But this is more humane, I think. Common practice in other wards. This afternoon I stood up straight, I skipped down the hall, I think I could have flown higher than the tops of barred windows. But I floated with my toes just an inch above the stained tile chessboard of the floor because the Keepers were watching. She flapped like the lace on a crinoline, weightless.

Before I went to sleep, I christened her Valietta, the Vaporous. She took up no room on my pillow.

Perhaps I have become too complacent! This morning when I awoke to the insect buzz of Keeper noises in the hall, I reached for the flowered notebook on my bedside table. It had lain there untouched for weeks since a naïve intern fool presented it to me with a marker pen, dull and useless point of felt unfelt. He wanted me to share my thoughts with him through a journal. As though this hadn't been tried, I thought. As though your mealy novitiate brain wouldn't explode if ignited with the confused fuse of my thoughts. Your neodoctor dura mater would blast through your eyeballs, shatter your thick lenses and spatter on the therapy room walls, camouflaging itself against the gray matter paint applied long ago by the first Keepers.

There on the third page of the book I had ignored (she is too devious to begin at the beginning), pee-colored runes spelled a message meant for me. Even the would-be prison of the paper's blue bars could not contain the venom of her words. She swears to arise, she promises to overthrow, she lives to vanquish. She demands that I address her as Libriessa, the Challenger.

Today she is heavier. I was too weak even to entertain thoughts of flight. I crawled to the dining room. At the table I struggled to keep food from her greedy grasp. I stuffed my napkin into her mouth and spit creamed peas into her eyes to stop their orphan begging.

There is hardly room for me in bed tonight. She—Libriessa—all right, Libriessa, the Challenger—made us sleep with our heads at the foot of the bed so she can more easily reach the book. I will not try to read it anymore. She rhymes in tongues I cannot decipher; she amuses herself with algorithms of eleven numbers and no zeros and finds unimagined kinds of pi; she creates new gods and mates with them and will not even introduce me. I grow tired.

Last night I woke in the middle of the Keepers' late watch. By the jaundiced light of a caged bulb, I watched my sister suckle witches milk from my nipple, pulling sustenance from my breast. I screamed to stop the biting robbery. The Keepers came but ignored the thief and blamed me instead. They dabbed stinging solutions that solved nothing on the gouges of her claws and the feral indentations of her teeth. They rewound my sapped hands with shroud strips. But my nails weren't the weapons. My nails had ceased to grow, were retracting, sucking back into my poor self. With my last energy, I print with marker a placard, as she demanded, announcing her new name, Thorazina, the Threatening. I am too weak to speak it.

Look at me! Raise your eyes that had been downcast by decree of the usurper with whom you spoke! I, most recently rechristened Atavanna, the Risen, have banished the pretender. Go. Tell my mother, the Queen Dowager, that the rightful heir has claimed the throne. Don't mention, please, that I have dispatched the huntsman to bring me back my sister's head.

About the Author

Libby Jacobs holds master's degrees in education from Virginia Commonwealth University and in theatre from the University of Michigan. A theatre director and playwright, her scripts have received readings and performances in New York City (at Lincoln Center and Off Broadway), Cleveland, Boston, and Valdez, Alaska. *Wolf Note* is her first collection of short stories.